Wil's Bones

Kevin Bowen

Engage Publishing
Port Townsend, Washington

This book is a work of fiction. Characters, names, institutions, statements and incidents are not intended to resemble or be attributed to any actual institution, entity or person, living or dead. Any such resemblance is entirely coincidental and the result of the author's imagination.

Biblical quotations are taken from the HOLY BIBLE: NEW INTERNATIONAL VERSION, 1978, by the International Bible Society.

Fiction (Adventure/Thriller)
ISBN: 1-930892-12-8
Library of Congress Card Number: 00-191018
Copyright Registration Number: TX5-258-987

Published by
Engage Publishing
P.O. Box 1452
Port Townsend, WA 98368
engagepublishing.com
wbinfo@engagepublishing.com
SAN: 253-2875

Printed in the Unites States of America

01 02 03 04 05 06 DP 8 7 6 5 4 3 2

This book is dedicated to Frank C. Roberts, Jr.

for his encouragement and because

he understood and added, "for all of us."

TABLE OF CONTENTS

Wil's Bones

Prologue

WIL

Smack! "Obey your father says the Lord," my drunken father bellowed as his hand recoiled from my stricken face. His other arm was around a woman who was not my mom. "Go to your room!"

Tears streamed down my reddened face as I turned and began up the stairs. The bruise was already beginning to form. I had only offered to help. Mom was normally able to calm him down and persuade the woman on his arm to go home. She was usually able to get Dad to lie still on the couch, after which he would finally pass out. But tonight, she was late getting home from her church meeting. I didn't know what to do, even though I'd been here before.

An hour later I heard screaming and yelling, followed by the door slamming. One of the voices was Mom's. A few minutes later a taxi picked up someone at our driveway. I guessed it was the woman. I cried most of the night. The few hours I did doze off weren't restful.

I absolutely did not want to get up for church. But it was Sunday, "the Lord's Day." That meant everyone in our house had to get up, put on their best clothes, and go to First Church of Hazel Dell.

I hated Sunday mornings. Fake smiles, plastic personalities. It was boring beyond belief. My brother, Mike, and I would have races to see who was the fastest at filling in all of the O's

1

on the church bulletin. We also made some pretty nice paper airplanes with the offering envelopes. The secret to winning any of the competitive games was to sit as far away from Dad as possible. The competition really took off when Dad would go up front to take the offering or to help serve communion with the other deacons. But even when he was in the same pew as we were, Dad rarely noticed us. He was usually too caught up in his *Amens* and *Hallelujahs* to pay attention to us boys, who were bored out of our skulls. And then there was Mr. Johnson.

Mr. Johnson was our Sunday school teacher. Dad and Mr. Johnson would go fishing together. On a few occasions I was allowed to go along. Mr. Johnson was a deacon, too. He and Dad would talk about the Bible and tithing and blacks in America. They would talk about liberals and abortionists and the FBI. But they hardly ever talked about my dad's drinking or his "other side." It amazed me. It seemed as if they avoided the subject, even though everybody knew about it.

When it did come up, Dad would lower his head and say in a very pious tone, "I messed up. But, I went to the cross and Jesus forgave me." Mr. Johnson seemed to accept this. So did Mom. I didn't.

No matter what Dad said or did, Mom would make excuses for him or take his side. There was only one time when Mom let on that it wasn't all roses between her and Dad. But Dad overheard her, and she changed her mind. She'd even make excuses for him after he'd beaten all three of us. Sometimes she'd blame me. But it wasn't my fault Dad got drunk and hit me. No way! And it didn't make sense for him to treat Mom the way he did. He was simply mean. But she just took it – over and over. It made me sick.

What made me the angriest was the way Mom and Dad would pretend to be the perfect couple at church the next day no matter what had occurred a few hours earlier. I despised the way Mom kowtowed to Dad's every wish. While I felt sorry for her, I didn't have pity for her because she never did anything to stop it, to stop him.

I hated my father. I hated his religion. And I hated the hypocrisy. I also knew I didn't have to believe his useless religion. For me, Christianity was all a bad joke people believed in for no reason. I never understood it. Dad used his religion like a mask. And Mom, she was even more religious than Dad. It was a way for her to make my dad happy. It was gross and it disgusted me.

By the time I was thirteen, I'd come to the conclusion that the best way to get back at my dad was to say I didn't believe. I did that one time.

The beating was severe, but for once, I knew my little body had beaten him. The wounds were mine, but so was the victory. Dad could not make me change my mind. Eventually, he could not even make me cry. From then on, I didn't say I believed or didn't believe. They knew where I stood on their "Jesus stuff" and that was my consolation. But this was only a partial victory. If I could convince Mom that Dad's Christian stuff was a joke, that would be the ultimate victory over my dad. I wanted this more than anything.

Death seldom ends anything.

Chapter 1

THE FUNERAL

Hypocrisy! This makes me sick! Wil could hardly stomach what was going on. From the sounds of it, one would think Wil's dad was Saint Peter himself.

Wil had been listening to the eulogies of the other deacons. The pastor had reiterated that they were there to remember what a "great man" Wil's dad had been and to celebrate that "Brother Robert Wilson, who died tragically in a car accident, has gone to be with God in Glory." Mr. Johnson's recountings of his fishing trips and theological conversations with Wil's dad were so seriously edited and embellished that the stories actually seemed interesting. But Wil knew there was no more truth in the stories than in the statements of a politician on the hot seat.

Wil's sickening feeling was magnified when his mom, Betty, stepped up to the microphone. The whole church grew quiet. Even the sobbing women gathered their composure to hear what was sure to be the apex of the service. Wil waited. What on earth was she going to say? His dad was dead. Her beatings would stop. She would get to sleep in sheets not soiled by another woman's perfume. Would she finally come clean?

Wil's memory of the evening his dad died was crystal clear. His dad came home drunker than a homesick sailor, with a new bimbo on his arm. Wil remembered seeing this woman at the church one Sunday a few weeks earlier and wasn't surprised.

There were the normal curt words between his mom and dad. A taxi picked up the bimbo. What followed was the worst fight Wil had ever seen his parents have.

It seemed his mom had had enough. Things were flying and his mom was on a roll. For some reason, Wil could not involve himself in this one. He had been beaten back and out of too many fights before. He retreated to the top of the stairs to watch the battle. At one point, Wil thought his dad was going to kill his mom. And then things changed.

Wil's mom, after taking a blow to the side of her face, stood and coldly said, "Either you leave this house now or I'll tell everyone the truth about your drinking and how you treat your family." Wil's dad stopped, sat down, and began to sob. This was new territory.

Then, rather than going after Wil's mom again, his dad did something Wil had never seen before. Instead of dragging her into the bedroom, where the screams would usually go silent, or forcing her to sit in a chair while he yelled, "Don't move or I'll break every stinkin' bone in your ugly body," he took the car keys and stumbled out of the house, slamming the door behind him.

Wil stared in disbelief and turned to his mom. Together they cleaned up the battlefield. Three hours later, they still hadn't heard anything from his dad. Wil had just fallen asleep when he heard his mom's voice.

"Wil, I'm worried. I called the tavern and your father isn't there. They haven't seen him." She was visibly distraught. "I think something's happened."

Wil wasn't sure what to do. He was torn between hoping something *had* happened and compassion for his pathetic mother. He got up without thinking, put his clothes on over his pajamas, and said, "Let's go."

They had driven for about five minutes in the direction of the tavern when they spotted lights off to the side of the road, partly hidden behind some overgrown blackberry bushes. They stopped. Wil got out of the car and walked in the direction of the lights. The tail end of his dad's car was barely sticking out of the slough. To the left of the car, his dad lay motionless, his head in a pool of blood that looked as if it had come out of his mouth. Wil shouted to his mom, "Stay there," and made his way back to the road. The next hour was a haze.

A policeman arrived. Wil recognized him as a deacon in the church.

Mr. Johnson arrived, which Wil perceived as strange.

The pastor arrived and then another deacon.

Then the ambulance.

Through it all no one talked to Wil, though they did talk to each other. No one asked Wil what had happened. His mom cried some. Then she showed the stamina Wil had repeatedly seen the morning after a rough night, her bruises camouflaged in a way that would make any Hollywood make-up artist proud.

Later that morning, Wil's mom called his older brother and told him about the accident. She told Wil through tearful eyes, "Mike won't be able to make it to the funeral. His college midterms are just three weeks away and he said the twenty-five-minute drive from Portland would take too much time away from his studies." Wil felt obligated to sympathize with his near-broken mom, but her sobbing caused her to excuse herself.

Wil's thoughts refocused on the present. From the pulpit, his mom began to talk, slowly at first and then more steadily. "He was a good man . . . and a servant of our Lord Jesus. . . . I loved him. . . . I miss him." As Wil's mom began to cry, so did many others. Then his mom began a series of religious praise and admiration statements about his dad.

Wil had to get up and leave.

People told Wil later how much it touched them when he left the sanctuary crying. He never told anyone that he barely made it to the toilet before the bile and vomit made its way out of his mouth.

Chapter 2

HOPE

Their lips had hardly parted. The tears on Hope's face were poorly disguised behind a facade of strength. Wil struggled to keep his emotions at bay. Her tears felt as if they could have been his. Wil knew this was goodbye.

Until this point, Hope and Wil had pretended this moment wouldn't come, even though it had been obvious from the day Wil accepted the position in Jerusalem. The evening strolls, the passionate embraces, the conversations about anything but the future – all avoided reference to this day when Wil would board the plane at Heathrow and probably never see Hope again.

It was almost three years since they had met in the small cafe in Paris. They were both away from Oxford for the holiday. Wil's French was good. However, his ear was for English and the sound of Hope's Wisconsin accent as she spoke on the phone in the booth behind his table caught his attention. When she walked from the phone booth, Wil took an unusual chance. He blurted out, "Wisconsin. Right?"

Wil was proud of himself. This was perhaps the first genuine "pass" he had ever made at a woman. Hope turned around, surprised to hear English for the first time in about three days.

"Yes," she said, acknowledging Wil's accurate but unsolicited inquiry.

And then, as if to stump and silence the unwanted interloper, she said, "But where in Wisconsin?"

Wil was taken aback by her response. Not wanting to look like an idiot, he tried to think of any city in Wisconsin. Instead he found himself staring, slack-jawed, at this woman.

She was beautiful. For some reason he couldn't look away from her eyes, which penetrated his. She had the most beautiful green eyes he had ever seen. And her neck . . . He was afraid he wasn't going to be able to think of anything. He was stunned. *What was in my wine?* he thought. His mind was blank. He mumbled "Oshkosh, Wisconsin." He didn't know why he said Oshkosh. It just slipped out.

"Pretty impressive," responded Hope as she stepped closer to him. "Are you a linguist?" Hope stuck her hand out straight, elbow locked, and grabbed Wil's hesitant hand. After shaking, or was it holding, her hand he pulled his back, slightly embarrassed that his sweaty palm had touched her soft skin. She smiled. "Hi. I'm Hope."

What in the world is going on here? was all Wil could muster in his mind as his soul responded to this person in front of him. And then his lips began to move, though they didn't seem to necessarily be connected to his brain. "I'm Wil . . . Wil Wilson . . . ummmm . . . I'm a student at Oxford. Uh . . . I'm here for the holiday and I overheard you talking on the phone and I'd been talking French for a day now and I heard your voice and then I remembered that I hadn't talked English for about a day and then I thought that maybe, since I'd been talking French all day and since I really prefer to talk in English and since I heard you speaking in English, I kind of thought you might be here by yourself and that . . ."

Hope interrupted his stammering and sat down at his table. She also had that look of Cupid interest, but she was not red in the face or blabbering. She inserted, as a way to let Wil catch his breath, "I'm studying at Oxford, too – literature and journalism."

Three hours, two bottles of wine, two cheese plates, and one napoleon later, they paused. Wil had never been involved with a woman before. He also had never felt so free. Within a month they were sharing an apartment.

It was now two years, ten and a half months later. Hope had one more year at Oxford. Wil had completed his work and it was time for his next chapter. But his plans hadn't accounted for Hope. He had grown to assume that she was part of his life. He had never thought about another person as much as he thought about Hope. The flowers he gave her were not simply to make her feel good. He couldn't help it. He'd get out of bed quietly, not because he thought she needed sleep, but so he could sit in the chair next to the bed and look at the most beautiful thing he had ever seen. He would make dinner, not merely because it was time to eat, but because he wanted to please her taste buds as much as he desired to please every other part of her. Hope was his love. There wasn't a before or an after. Hope was now.

Perhaps Wil didn't think about the future because of the fear he felt when he did. Perhaps he had avoided thinking about this day because it brought into conflict the two most powerful elements in his life – his love for Hope and his career ambitions. For the past three years, as his postgraduate studies progressed and Hope shared his life, he didn't have to think about this step. Everything was going great and the course was steady. There was no need to think about this day. But this day had finally come. The job in Jerusalem was what he had always wanted. It was, without a doubt, the best opportunity he could have ever imagined. He really didn't have a choice. Moreover, he pretended to himself, they would see each other again.

Wil walked down the ramp and began to question whether he was doing the right thing. His heart told him to stay. His footsteps slowed as he glanced back. Their eyes met one last time before the curve of the jetway took him out of sight.

As the plane began to lift off and the ground disappeared in the clouds, Wil knew he had said goodbye to Hope.

He cried.

Chapter 3

STEVE

There is something about Wil, thought Steve as he held the envelope. He reflected on the time they met, about fifteen years ago. Steve had taken his church's youth group for an outing at the ice rink. Wil had come along with a boy whose parents attended Steve's church. This was the only time Wil ever came to the youth group. That's one reason they both found it so peculiar that they had stayed in touch for so many years.

Steve remembered that Wil skated a little faster than the other kids. This was intriguing to Steve because it was Wil's first time. He just put on his skates and took off, careening around corners and bouncing off the railings. Some of his falls were amazing. On Wil's third time around the rink, he was goofing off with his friend and trying to skate backwards. He lost his balance and spun around, kind of tiptoeing, tight-roping, running and falling all at one time. He almost pulled it off, but a little girl and her mother got in his path and, when he jumped to avoid them, he smacked into the Zamboni ice machine parked in the corner. Steve hesitated about ten seconds to see if he needed to call for an ambulance. Wil rolled to his knees, shaking his head. Slowly and more determined than ever, he pulled himself up and started around the rink again. Two laps later Wil had his speed up, and the collisions with hard objects continued. By the end of the day, Wil had become a pretty good skater. (The next day at the church staff meeting, Steve inquired about the church's liability insurance policy.)

In between the horsing around and near-death experiences, Steve got in about twenty laps with Wil. They hit it off. Neither can remember what they talked about. Steve simply remembers really liking this kid. He was disappointed when Wil didn't show up at the youth group meeting the following Wednesday, or for that matter, ever again.

Then, one Thursday night about twelve weeks later, Wil phoned.

"Do you like punk rock?"

When they got together, Steve listened to Wil's tape. Steve found the music rather obnoxious, though the words were interesting. Wil's music wasn't simply the mere noise the other kids in Steve's youth group listened to. There was drive and rebellion and strategy in the songs. His music matched his eyes.

At first they talked on the phone. Later they talked over an occasional soda at McDonald's. Wil always refused Steve's invitations to the youth group.

In Steve's five years of youth work following seminary he had never developed a relationship with any other kid that was as deep and as intellectually stimulating. Wil was brilliant and his knowledge of the Christian religion was far beyond that of his peers. Nevertheless, Wil was adamant that he wasn't a Christian. He would tell Steve, "I don't believe that Jesus is what you Christians make him out to be." Steve had met many people who articulated Wil's position. He never met anyone who said it with as much intensity, rebellion, or determination.

"You know, he hasn't changed that much . . . even after all these years," Steve muttered to himself. He smiled and opened the letter.

Chapter 4

LETTER TO STEVE

HEBREW UNIVERSITY JERUSALEM
WILLIAM WILSON, PH.D., M.A.A.
PROFESSOR OF ARCHAEOLOGICAL RESEARCH

7/21/90

Steve:

Thanks for the historical encyclopedia set. I used the library's copy on nearly a daily basis when I was preparing my dissertation. The fact that I had it practically memorized seemed to impress my examiners when I sat for my orals. In any case, my student budget didn't allow me to buy one, so your generous gift is much appreciated.

I left London last week for Jerusalem. I can hardly wait to get going on my work here at Hebrew University. I will be fairly busy with my teaching load, but the opportunity to be in this area for digs, research, and overall access is quite exciting.

My article on first-century Palestine was published in *Archaeology Today*. The article has turned out to be positive for my career. Apparently my minor in English has enabled me to write in a more palatable manner than many of my colleagues. Three foundations have agreed to fund my research project on the topography and culture of first-century Palestine. The funny thing is that the two largest donors are an evangelical conservative group out of Atlanta and a Muslim religious group from Saudi. I wonder if I should plan on sending out one generic status letter? Somehow, I don't think that would be wise. Anyway, it doesn't matter to me. I'm just thrilled with the opportunity. My four previous trips were so fulfilling that this long-term placement is sure to be even more so.

I broke up with Hope. She really wanted to get married. I didn't, even though I think I loved her. We parted on pretty good terms, though deep down inside, I'm pretty sure she is ticked off at me. She will probably be better off without me anyway. She has one more year before she graduates and then she wants to return to the States. With my planning to be in Israel for the next number of years, we were headed for a conflict anyway.

By the way, congratulations on your new church! I find it kind of odd that a small-town boy like you ends up in New York City. Quite a change from Hazel Dell! There certainly will be more for you to do and see in New York than in Hazel Dell. I hope it is another positive experience for you. In any case, you still have the nicest woman in the world by your side. Give Wendy and little William my regards. I still can't believe you named your son after me.

Wish you the best.

Wil

Chapter 5

Mom

Wil picked up the phone to call his mom. It was Sunday morning in Hazel Dell, Washington, and he knew she would be at the church.

He had not forgiven her for the funeral. He had not forgotten her allegiance to his dad even as he beat them. Time had only slightly softened his feelings toward her, even though she had changed, no longer under his dad's influence. Wil's anger ran deep. It wasn't so much at his mom but, in the absence of his father, she was the nearest thing.

Wil's mom had come to accept Wil's anger, but it hurt her – deeply. She also had accepted his hatred of Christianity, or what he called "Dad's religion." During the few times they had seen each other after Wil left for college a dozen years ago, Wil's mom had tried to let him know she loved him. She even tried to apologize for putting up with his dad. But Wil's heart was still too hard and her attempts at reconciliation met only wooden responses.

It had been nearly two years since they had spoken. Wil's mom had spent two days with Wil and Hope in London. It was obvious that Wil's mom liked Hope – a lot. She also didn't hide how pleased she was to see Wil so happy.

Wil dialed.

"I'm sorry I'm not here right now. Please leave a message

17

at the tone and I'll call you back. Have a nice day!" *Beeeeeep.*

"Hi Mom. It's Wil. All's well. I've been in Jerusalem for about a month now. Hope and I broke up before I left London. Things are going well for me. I received some more funding for my work in Palestine. Please don't be too upset, but I won't be home for Christmas again this year. Take care."

Wil hung up the phone. He was glad to have that out of the way.

Chapter 6

HOPE AND NEWCASTLE

Hope had worked for the *Boston Globe* for nearly nine years when she received the call from Congressman Henry Newcastle. She had known him for a number of years. They had met at a few functions and eventually grew to mutually respect each other, though their relationship was always a little peculiar because of Hope's position with the paper. She had voted for him in the last four elections and would have voted for him the previous four except that her age, her overseas studies, and her low regard for the American political system had prevented her. Her solace was that he had won each time anyway.

Hope had done well at the *Globe*. She was something of a marvel among her colleagues, not only for the quality of her writing, but also for her ability to separate herself from whatever issue she was covering. She was good. However, as is often the case, good isn't enough. Hope had climbed the ladder, not by sleaze or merely hard work, but because, along with her talent, she had the ability to get powerful people to like her even though she didn't always like them.

People couldn't help being drawn to her and wanting her on their team. This was evident the first time Hope explained to her editor's boss, with a completely submissive tone, how the editor's modifications of her article on the city's recycling system were "appreciated." Hope explained that she truly appreciated her editor's reminding her that journalistic objectivity was not always the best tactic. She acknowledged, with a subtle cynicism, that this was a failure resulting from her training at Oxford. She praised the way her editor had taken her overly serious article about a very important issue and made it an effective form of minimalist humor.

With a grin borrowed from the Cheshire cat from *Alice in Wonderland*, she said, "My editor's version communicates the point *much* more effectively."

At first Hope thought the boss was going to fire her for her satirical candor and insubordination. She felt fortunate to leave the inner sanctum without that result. Instead, the editor's name replaced hers in the byline of the seriously modified article and she received a promotion, a larger office, and an invitation to staff meetings. Within a year she had received a Pulitzer nomination and climbed further within the *Globe*'s internal power structure. Her colleagues pegged her as someone who was undoubtedly going to have a very successful career.

The call from the congressman's office was unexpected. Newcastle was serious and vague as he asked her to join him for dinner that evening. She accepted. It could be a good story.

Hope sat at the white-linen-covered table looking at the stately gentleman across from her. She still had no clue as to why the congressman wanted to meet with her. He was too old, and his wife too powerful, for him to try anything stupid. He had recently come through a difficult election in which the press, her included, commented on the ineffective and diffident nature of his campaign.

The waiter, white cloth draped over his arm, asked if she cared for a cocktail. Hope ordered a martini. The congressman ordered a ginger ale.

"Ginger ale?" Hope raised an eyebrow as the waiter walked away.

"My wife. The rules. When I'm with a woman, only non-alcoholic beverages."

They laughed, though Hope wasn't completely sure if the congressman was joking or telling the truth. She thought about the few times she had met his wife, and concluded he was telling the truth.

"Hope." Newcastle leaned forward, putting an end to the laughter. "As you know, we've had some changes on my staff as I've tried to get people to understand my message."

"Uh huh." Hope began to look for a pad and pencil in her purse, still not sure what was up.

He reached forward and lightly touched her purse and hand. "Please."

This was going to be off the record. Hope was setting down her purse when her cocktail arrived. She took an exceptionally large sip, truly baffled.

"You see, Hope," Newcastle continued, "I've been in Washington long enough to know there's little that happens in government that isn't the result of someone manipulating the system to his own advantage." He paused as if trying to muster the courage to continue. "However, this week I had a meeting with the senator."

"Senator Brown?" queried Hope, knowing it was the only senator he could have meant.

"Yes." Newcastle had intentionally avoided using the senator's name. "In that meeting, I was informed that some of my positions have to change because they are no longer consistent with the views of certain key people in the state." The congressman sat back and sighed. He leaned in again, closer this time.

"You see, there's some new blood in Massachusetts that has

decided there's lots of money to be made if I'd change my stance on some issues. It seems that the desire for money in order to maintain office has finally prevailed among almost all of my colleagues – of both parties. I know money's influence isn't new. You know that."

The congressman thought about this statement of the obvious, and acknowledged, "Heck, everyone knows that! But what's so disturbing is that the people the senator is working for make Al Capone look like an angel. And, as you know, all politics in this state, regardless of which party, start and end with Senator Brown."

"So," Hope responded. "What does this have to do with me – or with the *Globe*?"

She meant it. Everyone in Massachusetts knew that Senator Harold Brown was the most powerful person in the state. Everyone knew he was shady, though he came off as a saint. Even the *Globe*'s editorial board supported him, which to Hope wasn't necessarily a great credential but it did make Newcastle's comments more unexpected.

Newcastle looked directly into Hope's eyes. She was startled by his intensity.

"This has nothing to do with the *Globe*. It has to do with you."

This made Hope a little nervous. She waited in silence, out of respect for the sincerity and vulnerability of this man she had grown to admire. She emptied her glass and subtly signaled the waiter for another martini.

"Here's the situation," Newcastle continued. "I've been in politics for a long time. I've tried to serve my country to the best of my ability – and maintain my honor. I've taken a number of risks and, fortunately, most of them have paid off. I've made some enemies and have usually prevailed against their zealous, intrusive agendas."

Hope recalled Newcastle's ongoing and well-known feud with Congressman Jerry Jones, a conservative from South Carolina.

"I've tried to do what I thought was right."

Hope began to feel like a priest in a confessional.

"During this last election – which, to my surprise, I ended up winning – I tasted the other side, the new side of politics in this state. I hated it. I now have a choice of complying and maintaining my office, which will result in my wife hanging her head in shame when I come home, or I can say 'no' to the money and to Senator Brown and his cronies. But what good is 'no' if I end up fading away and letting the corrupt money-grubbers win?" The congressman paused, but not long enough to let Hope answer his rhetorical question.

"I've decided that I'm going to fight. I realize the congressional election results are hardly out of the news, but tomorrow I will announce that I'm going to challenge Senator Brown for the Senate seat in two years."

Hope stared in mute surprise.

"I'm going to go public with it now so I'll have plenty of time to recover after the initial salvo of attacks hits me. I want plenty of time to restore my image, which I'm certain will be destroyed within days of my announcement."

"Congressman," Hope interjected, "what does this have to do with me?"

Without taking a breath Newcastle said, "I want you to be my chief of staff and coordinate my campaign."

Hope nearly choked on her olive.

The congressman didn't blink.

"Hope, you're honest. You're good. You write better than anyone I've ever read. You're fresh and untainted. You have a stellar reputation. You're safe. Hope, I need you to help me do this."

"Why should I?" Hope asked softly, not so much looking

for a philosophical or moral justification, but trying to convince herself this wasn't the craziest thing she had ever heard.

"You probably shouldn't," Newcastle responded frankly. "However, if there's one thing I've learned over the past nine years, both watching you and reading your columns, it's that you like a challenge and you particularly like it when you know you're right. Hope, what I'm doing is the right thing. If I don't do this, Brown will so soil the system in this state that any person who doesn't sign on with him won't stand a chance, regardless of what party they run under. I don't want that to happen. I can't let it happen. Will you help me?"

Hope was stymied and the congressman knew it. Rather than press the issue, and in order to forestall an immediate negative reply, Newcastle added. "Don't answer now. Think about it."

The waiter arrived. "Have you decided?" They both looked at their menus, grateful for the distraction.

"What do you recommend?" asked Newcastle.

"The *tournedos* of beef are marvelous."

The conversation turned to other subjects for the rest of dinner.

Hope got home around nine o'clock. After a sleepless night, she submitted her resignation the next morning.

Hope convinced the congressman it would be wise to hold off on his announcement for a few weeks, at least while they worked on their plan. Within one month, she was in D.C. running the congressman's office and working on the plan for his election.

Chapter 7

E-MAIL FROM STEVE

To:	Wil (Wilson@InstPalRes.net)
From:	Steve (PastorSteve@DC.net)
Subject:	Congratulations
Date:	4/30/99

Wow! Why didn't you tell me? I don't know too much about your field of expertise but, from what the *Times* said, the Medal of Achievement from the International Institute of Science is quite an accomplishment. You told me about your induction into the National Academy of Science a few years ago, but I didn't know you also won the Distinguished Service Award from the International Archaeological Society. You've amassed quite the trophy collection. Congratulations, Wil!

I tried to call you at the Institute in Jerusalem, but Beth said you were on a dig and were not reachable. She gave me your e-mail address. I understand you weren't available for the announcement either? From what she told me, some of the officials from the International Institute were a little perturbed with your response to their selection of you. Did you really just send a telegram saying, "Thank you. The funds will be helpful in my research"? Why does that not surprise me? Even prestigious international recognition and a quarter million dollars in award money didn't cause you to stop for a break! One has to wonder if there are many people in the world who are as dedicated to their work as you are. I only hope you are around long enough to realize what an accomplishment you've made. I suppose, as you've frequently said, you "don't really care." For what it's worth, I care, and I am proud of you.

Wendy and I have settled in quite well here in D.C. We had a great eight years in New York. The church grew, the membership was committed, my assistant was poised to take over, and I was ready for a new challenge. After William's death in the car accident, we also thought a change would be good. My first year at Trinity Church went exceptionally well. I must admit, I still find it odd to be a counselor and preacher to so many "important people" like congressmen, ambassadors and senators. But we really are happy here.

Again, Wil, congratulations. As much as I am not thrilled with what is behind your drive and dedication to your work, I am happy for you and that you are proving to be so successful in your field.

Best Wishes.

Steve

Chapter 8

A NOTE FROM HOPE

(HANDWRITTEN)

May 11, 1999

Dear Wil,

Are you surprised to hear from me? I read the news of your award in the *Washington Times* last week. I'm happy for you. By the sound of it, you are accomplishing some of your dreams.

I have tried to stop thinking about you, but seeing your picture in the paper set me back a bit. You probably think I'm a nut to write you this letter. I guess I figured you wouldn't mind, since we agreed to stay in touch when you left for Jerusalem. I feel as though I'm forfeiting a staring contest after nine years.

So much has happened since we last saw each other. I went to work for the *Boston Globe* following my return to the States. People say I was pretty good. I didn't win any big awards like you, but my series on welfare reform was nominated for a Pulitzer. And then, a little over a year ago, I became chief of staff for Congressman Newcastle of Massachusetts and I moved to D.C. We're preparing for a very contentious senatorial race in a few months.

I know – you probably can't believe I'm in politics. Truthfully, neither can I. But Congressman Newcastle stands for so much of what I believe in. He's trying to win an impor-

tant battle against greed and power involving a dangerous senator. When he asked for my help, I couldn't refuse.

I miss you, Wil. I wish you the best. If you are ever in D.C.,
give me a call.

Hope
2897 Virginia Avenue
Washington DC, 00676
202-555-7985

Chapter 9

BETH'S CALL

Wil shook the dust off his clothes and sat at his desk. He reached for the stack of mail that had accumulated over the past month. Napoleon, his huge and obviously happy tabby cat, climbed into Wil's lap, after dropping Wil's slippers by the chair. Each time Napoleon performed this feat, Wil chuckled in disbelief at how far his feline had come since the days of consuming shoes when Wil and Hope lived together in London. Shaking his head, he remembered with a smile how they named this stray cat after the dessert they had shared the day they met.

Wil tossed most of the mail unopened into the overflowing wastepaper basket under his desk. Once in a while he would mumble something in response to a return address. He hesitantly set aside one letter and headed to the shower.

Half clothed, not quite making it to the shower, he returned to his desk, sat down, and picked up the letter again. "D.C.!" he mumbled as he stared off into space. He was talking to the cat, which had again climbed into his lap. "I can't believe she's in D.C.!" He hadn't heard from Hope since Heathrow, though he thought about her all the time.

He held the letter for several minutes before he reached for his letter opener, sliced the end of the envelope, and slid its contents into his right hand. He paused again. He wasn't quite sure he wanted to know what it said. *What if —*

The phone rang.

"Dr. Wilson?" inquired the voice at the other end of the line. "Dr. Wilson, thank goodness you're home."

"Why thank you, Beth," Wil responded warmly to his secretary, confidante, friend, and comrade in battle. He couldn't help but notice her relief. "What's wrong?"

"Nothing's wrong, Dr. Wilson. It's just, this one is so big I'm having a hard time figuring out what to do." That meant something to Wil. The numerous invitations, offers, and requests he received had turned Beth into one of the best assets a person in demand could ever dream of wanting. She could say no to anyone, make him or her feel good, make Wil look great, and still keep Wil's schedule clear for his own endeavors. If Beth was rattled, Wil knew something unusual must be going on.

"What is it, Beth?"

"Well, Dr. Wilson, it seems your presence is required at a meeting at the American Embassy this afternoon. They would not tell me anything else. And I mean I tried. I informed them you were not available. When they told me a contingent of security personnel would arrive at your home around three o'clock today, I realized this might be important."

"Jeez," muttered Wil as he tried to guess what in the world was going on. It was disconcerting that Beth seemed so flustered. Wil had met Beth prior to starting work at the Institute. She was hard to miss – five feet four inches tall, rich black hair, and eyes that were a lustrous gray. Her complexion was lighter than most Palestinians' and her accent, perhaps due to her schooling overseas, was almost non-existent. Wil had met her while visiting a respected, now retired, colleague at the Institute. When Wil moved from Hebrew University to the Institute of Palestinian Research and occupied the office vacated by his retiring colleague, Beth came with the territory. He knew how fortunate he was to have her on his staff.

People often wondered why Wil never took more than a professional interest in Beth. They enjoyed each other's company and in many ways functioned like a couple. But, after a painful divorce, Beth had pledged never to get involved again. Wil had lost all interest in women and love the day he left Hope behind at Heathrow. They also had a high sense of vocational respect for each other.

Wil and Beth behaved more like siblings than anything else. This was apparent when Wil would badger her to go out with one of his colleagues, who never failed to notice what a special person Beth was. They would plead with Wil for the favor. He tried – but never prevailed. Beth was not easily manipulated and few things could rattle her. Being stumped by a phone call demanding Wil's presence was truly out of the ordinary.

There was a period of silence.

"I guess I'd better go then," Wil said, more curious than upset.

"I think so." Beth's tone was that of a loyal comrade ready to join him in battle.

Wil hung up. The beeping on his watch told him he had only thirty minutes. He reluctantly put down the unread letter and headed again to the shower.

Time changes. Sometimes.

Chapter 10

DRAFTED

Wil sat next to one of the three uniformed escorts. The other two were in front. They were Israeli secret police. What could be so important? Had he done something wrong? Had he really ticked someone off?

The car was silent except for the radio playing music that, even after his years in Israel, Wil had not yet learned to enjoy. One of the men held a gun in his lap. Except for an occasional comment about traffic or directions to the embassy, no one spoke. They were aware of Wil's command of their language, which they had spoken with him when they arrived at his door. Wil thought the whole thing odd. His palms were damp. What was he nervous about?

On the drive through Jerusalem Wil couldn't help but notice the hundreds of placard-carrying citizens of this troubled yet wonderful city. They were protesting the upcoming visit by the Secretary of State. She was to facilitate a peace agreement brokered by the U.S. government. The plan was to be ratified by the Palestinians and Israelis and, according to the pollsters, demonstrated the U.S. President's skills in international affairs. This, along with the President's strong gains in recent months with Christian voters, had managed to move him ahead in the polls. If there were no major surprises and the President could hold onto his new Christian supporters, he was guaranteed another four years in the White House in the upcoming election.

It was clear to Wil that, regardless of what the leaders were doing, consensus was not in the making in the hearts of the people of this land. This place was a political time bomb that would explode now and then – and never go away. Wil had grown accustomed to the ebb and flow of the politics involving this land. His knowledge of Israel's history informed him that these conflicts had gone on for centuries. Regardless of what happened in the polls or on paper, the conflicts were not going to be solved. In fact, this was part of the basis of his prize-winning work.

He noticed one particularly hostile placard cursing the upcoming visit of the Secretary. Wil reflected on the many leaders who had come to this city over the centuries as kings, governors, conquerors, or emissaries of hostile forces. He wondered what a Roman Caesar in the first century, a period Wil knew almost better than the present, would have done to citizens who expressed themselves in such a way. His studies suggested that the messages on the signs certainly would not have been as unfriendly. At the same time, he realized that in many ways, this place and its issues had not changed much over the past two thousand years.

"Here's our paperwork," the driver said in remarkably clear English to the Marine guard at the embassy gate. The guard let them pass without further questioning. They drove Wil into the compound, where they stopped in front of the main building. The uniformed escort in the front passenger seat got out and opened Wil's door. The driver and another embassy official exchanged a few words as Wil got out of the car. He wished he had been able to hear them. As he started to ask the embassy official what this was about, he noticed that the car he had arrived in was leaving. He wondered how he was going to get home – or if he would get home at all.

"Please follow me, Dr. Wilson," said the official.

Wil followed him up the stairs and into the building. The Marine guards recognized the man who, with a gesture, indicated that Wil was with him. They allowed the two to stroll unattended up the stairs, down a hallway, and into a meeting room. Five other people were in the room. One of them, a young, red-headed male staff member offered Wil coffee and left the room. Wil took a seat.

They were waiting. It was like being in an elevator or a doctor's waiting room. Everyone is there for the same thing, but the rules are that no one can talk.

"Does anyone have any idea what's going on here?" Wil couldn't stand the silence.

Wil's violation of the code of conduct caught them by such surprise that they all responded simultaneously. "No!" Perhaps it was the oddity of people unknown to each other saying "no" in perfect timing, or maybe it was the tension they all felt, but this unexpected unison raised a brief chuckle from the group. Then they fell silent again, with uneasy smiles lingering and eventually fading.

"So," said Wil. "I'm Wil Wilson. I've been taken hostage by the Israeli secret police and am being held in a meeting room in the U.S. Embassy with four strangers. How's your day been?"

A few smiles returned. The older woman, who seemed the most out of place, surrounded by peculiar-looking men, extended her hand toward Wil to shake. She was Israeli, though she appeared to be of Palestinian descent. "Hello, I am Sarah Shner. I also have no idea what is going on. But when I got here ten minutes ago I was told we would be getting started in ten minutes."

Wil shook her hand. "Getting started at what?" He asked, relieved that someone was talking to him.

"I don't really kno–"

The door swung open and in walked the U.S. ambassador and a woman who looked to be in her mid-thirties. The woman was striking in appearance, tall and thin with chiseled features. She looked like someone you did not want to cross. Accompanying them was a colonel in the Israeli secret police. Some of those at the table began to stand. The ambassador asked everyone to remain seated. Not expecting the ambassador himself, Wil sat dumbfounded.

"As some of you already know, I am Ambassador Philip Worthington. I want to apologize for the way we had to get you all together. We are facing a very difficult situation. We need your help. I hope it will make more sense as things are explained to you. But first allow me to introduce you to each other."

The ambassador went around the table, which was much larger than the group needed, and introduced each of the five "hostages" to the others. Sarah Shner, the older Israeli woman, turned out to be the Director of Tourism for the Israeli government. A short, stout German man with a balding head and round glasses was introduced as a professor at Hebrew University. A medium-built, dark-haired man in the crumpled suit was a professor from the University of California on loan to Tel Aviv University. Both men were introduced as experts on Middle East terrorism with a focus on groups active in and around Jerusalem. The fourth person, a tall man with a dark, ruddy complexion, was the head of the Jerusalem Transportation Department. Wil was introduced as "the world's premier expert on Palestinian archaeology and the author of a recent book on the history, topography and archaeology of Jerusalem."

The ambassador thanked them for their cooperation, and then introduced the two people he said would be heading up a special project.

"Kathreen Steele is a special assistant for the United States

Department of State. Colonel Jakob Rabin is with the Israeli secret police. Colonel Rabin will inform you about why we called you here." With that the ambassador excused himself from the room, explaining that other matters demanded his immediate attention.

Steele wasted no time in getting started. Her clipped words and concise imparting of information matched her clear and defined features. She and the colonel were co-leaders, but it was obvious that Steele would be calling the shots.

In the next hour Wil and the rest of the group learned of a terrorist plot to kill the Unites States' Secretary of State during her upcoming visit to Jerusalem. Each of them had been specifically "selected," Steele explained, because of their knowledge of the area, the tourist sites, the geography, and the terrorist groups involved. The terrorists planned to target a major tourist area where the Secretary, American citizens, and "Jewish occupiers" would all be impacted at the same time.

The colonel, who had been quiet to this point, said, "We were concerned that this group might be threatening nuclear or chemical means. We now have reason to believe that this is not the case."

"Reason to believe?" inquired Wil, alarmed.

The colonel continued. "It seems the group behind this effort is a new splinter group that recently broke off from Hamas. They are still small and have not had time to get their hands on such ordnance. We believe they are planning either a series of dynamite explosions or one large explosion near the Temple Mount in Jerusalem. We have ruled out areas occupied predominantly by Palestinians as well as areas where the Secretary would not reasonably be expected to go. It is strongly suspected that their plan involves the support of employees, or an employee, of one of the major tourist areas. We believe they plan to position explosives where they will affect either what the Secretary is doing or impact her directly."

"So . . ." Wil drawled the unspoken consensus of the other four invited guests, "cancel the trip!"

"That is *not* an option." Steele took over from the colonel somewhat curtly and with more volume than was necessary. "The President and the leaders of the Israeli government and the Palestinian Council believe this visit is possibly one of the most important moments in the peace process. It is not generally known that originally the President himself was going to attend. However, on the recommendation and consent of the Palestinian and Israeli leadership, the decision was made to send the Secretary. The Secretary *is* coming, and our job – and our request of you – is to prevent a disaster."

"I'm an archaeologist for heaven's sake," retorted Wil. "What in the world can I do to help?"

Steele leaned across the table, forcing the colonel to step back. He was in the way of her intense communication with Wil. She had anticipated Wil's objection.

"Dr. Wilson, is it true that you recently discovered a new, hidden chamber in one of the caves where the Dead Sea Scrolls were found?"

"Well . . ." Wil hedged as he wondered where this line of questioning was headed. "Yes, but a chamber is a bit of an over-statement."

"Unless I am mistaken," continued Steele, "you received special permission to dig in a cave that had been searched over and over by countless archaeologists, geologists, and scholars for years."

"And all I found was another cave with a few pieces of unremarkable, broken pottery shards." Wil finished the story slightly embarrassed with the outcome of his dig and wanting to get a straight answer. "And what does that have to do with this current situation?"

Steele turned to Shner, who had not said a word since introducing herself to Wil before the meeting. "When was the last time a focused dig was permitted in one of the major tourist areas such as the Church of the Holy Sepulchre or the Garden of Gethsemane or the site commonly called 'the Garden Tomb'?"

"Oh, it has been years since anything significant has been done," responded Shner, seemingly pleased she had been asked something to which she knew the answer. "For one thing, we have been reluctant to close off any of the sites, since we believe it is our duty to allow the many pilgrims and tourists to visit these places they have journeyed so far to see."

"And you wouldn't collect the precious tourist money if the sites were closed," muttered the professor from the University of California. Smiles briefly appeared on the faces of some of the people around the table, a large one on Wil's.

"And," continued Shner unmoved, "those areas that are easily accessible have been gone over with a – how do you say it? – a comb with small teeth."

This time, she was interrupted by Steele. "Similar to the cave where Dr. Wilson discovered the hidden chamber?"

"This is insane," grumbled Wil loudly enough for everyone to hear.

"Is it really, Dr. Wilson?"

"What?" Wil knew the answer to his next question would be no. "Are you saying we're going to do some digging at the famous tourist sites?"

Wil had tried over and over during his time in Israel to get permission to do some digs in these areas, particularly around the supposed tombs of Jesus. Each time he was denied, usually for some lame reason he had learned to translate as, "No, because we don't want to bother the tourists." However, the powers that be always denied this when he accused them of petty shortsightedness.

"Yes." This time Colonel Rabin responded. Steele smirked as if she had trumped Wil's ace.

Wil sat up, astonished. What had he just heard?

"We have reason to believe that one of these sites is going to be used as a staging area for the terrorist attack and that the terrorists are working with site staff. It's likely they have either discovered a hidden chamber similar to the one Dr. Wilson found or that they are planning to stage their attack from one of the many restricted areas off-limits to the public.

Wil had been launched out of the room into another dimension. Could this be for real? Was he actually going to explore some of these restricted sites?

"But the Secretary is to be here in two weeks," pointed out the transportation expert, who now better understood his role. He was also beginning to dread the next two weeks even more than he had when he first heard about the Secretary's visit.

"Perhaps y'all now understand the urgency with which we called you together," concluded Steele, uncharacteristically letting a southern accent show. It was her attempt to appear friendlier and less rigid.

"So what do we do?" asked Wil, suddenly interested.

"Well," answered Steele with the closest thing to a smile she could muster. She was prepared to get to work. "D'you have any ideas?"

Chapter 11

THE SITES

Wil's mind was still spinning seven days after being drafted into this effort. His past was crashing into his future. His reason for going into archaeology was ceasing to be a college kid's dream and was becoming a man's reality. He remembered how it began.

He was a junior in college and getting ready to go to the Student Union Building with his roommate, Scott, to hear a speaker named Keith McDonald. Wil couldn't believe he was going. Not only did he have a ton of studying to do, he didn't want to listen to this guy.

"Ready?" asked Scott, preparing for another verbal jousting match at which he had become expert. Wil had seen him in action many times before. He would wear orange on Saint Patrick's Day, wave Soviet flags at Republican rallies, and pretend to be a *Playboy* photographer soliciting models at women's rights marches. One time he caught a powerful senator completely off guard with a question about his personal financial dealings. The next day a photo in the newspaper showed the seasoned politician, eyes nearly popping, pointing his finger at a calm and normal-looking kid. Scott boasted for years that he had cost that senator the election.

Nothing was sacred to Scott. He was a nice guy, but he

could never pass up a chance to be contrary with anybody about anything. Wil could usually beat him in any one-on-one debate, but no one was better in public than Scott.

The first day Wil saw the flyers posted in the Student Union Building, he knew Scott would not be able to pass on this one. The flyer read:

Christian Apologist and Scholar
Keith McDonald
Speaking on The Resurrection of Jesus and
What It Means to You.

Wil said "No" to his roommate at least fifteen times. It was only when Scott promised to buy him a tank of gas that he finally conceded.

So, here he was. At least the meeting wasn't in a tent with schlocky organ music in the background. There were so many preppie-looking Christians in the crowd that his roommate was salivating even more than normal. Wil could hear Scott mutter under his restrained but plotting demeanor, "This is going to be great. This is going to be great. This is going to be great!"

Wil was beginning to think that a tank of gas wasn't enough.

"Hi, I'm Bill and this is Jenny," said a guy in khakis and a polo shirt.

Oh Jeez, we've been noticed! thought Wil, almost out loud. He politely turned to the smiling students.

"Hi." Wil grinned compliantly on behalf of himself and his roommate. But when he looked for backup he noticed that Scott had already made his move to the front of the auditorium.

"Isn't this great?" bubbled Jenny, excited about the speaker.

Wil grinned again, feeling foolish.

"We've been trying to get Keith here for over a year," said

Bill. "His books have really been selling well and we thought it would be fantastic to have him here in person."

"Oh." Wil couldn't quite figure out how he had ended up in this conversation.

"Have you read any of his books?" asked Jenny, who began to pick up on Wil's body language that he didn't share their enthusiasm.

"No. Actually, I just came with my roommate." Wil had hoped for a, "So, where is your roommate?" or "Really?" or some other opening that would allow him to politely say, "Oh, he's over there. I'd better catch up with him," at which time he planned to exit the conversation. No such luck.

"Is your roommate a Christian?" asked Bill.

"Uhh . . . I wouldn't say that." Wil was trying to come up with another plan.

"Why'd you guys come?" asked Jenny with a friendly smile.

Wil was saved when an event coordinator stepped onto the stage and began to speak. Wil took full advantage of the distraction. "Y'know, I'd really like to keep talking with you, but I'd better catch up with my roommate. It looks like things are getting ready to start." He made his escape.

Sure enough, the crowd was beginning to settle as one of the organizers began to welcome everybody and gesture that it was time to sit down.

"Thanks, buddy!" Wil said as he elbowed Scott and settled into the chair his roommate had designated for him.

"For what?"

"For ditching me! I almost got sucked into a religious conversation with two preppie Christians!"

Scott wasn't listening. He was too busy sizing up the situation. Wil sat back, prepared to endure about forty-five minutes of lecture by a guy he didn't know about or care about before the fireworks would begin. To him it was like being forced to listen to a sportscaster before a professional wrestling match when you're not at all interested in professional wrestling. He figured the best thing to do was endure and try to enjoy. At least he had a front-row seat. He sat back and hoped it would be over quickly.

Keith McDonald introduced himself. He told the audience about his years as a prosecuting attorney in New York. He cracked a few lawyer jokes and then began to tell how he had set out, at one point in his life, to disprove Christianity.

Wil looked up, suddenly attentive. McDonald explained how the central factor in his conversion to Christianity had been the resurrection of Jesus. He quoted a passage from the Bible:

> And if Christ has not been raised, our preaching is useless and so is your faith. More than that, we are then found to be false witnesses about God, for we have testified about God that he raised Christ from the dead. . . . And if Christ has not been raised, your faith is futile; you are still in your sins. Then those who have fallen asleep in Christ are lost. If only for this life we have hope in Christ, we are to be pitied more than all men.

Wil didn't hear anything else for the next forty minutes. He sat in amazement, contemplating that he had been handed the piece of the puzzle he'd been missing. Five years after his dad's death, Wil had not forgotten his hatred for his dad's religion. His mom's continued attendance at the church and her persistence in her beliefs only served to further infuriate Wil. He was determined to bring down his dad's Christianity. But until now he didn't know how he was going to do it. This speaker, at a lecture he didn't want to attend, had given him his plan. He would disprove the resurrection. He would finally be able to refute his dad's religion. He would destroy Christianity. *He would find Jesus' bones.*

"Excuse me." Wil was jarred out of his reflection as Scott stood up to ask his first question. "You keep talking about a loving God. How can there be a loving, all-powerful God who lets people suffer like they do in the killing fields of Cambodia?" Scott smirked, believing he had scored a home run.

"Good question. Thank you for asking it."

That certainly wasn't the response Wil or Scott expected.

"That's also a question that isn't going to be fully answered here or in the near future. I'm not afraid to admit there are many things about God's interaction with people I don't understand. But this I do know. The bullets killing those people, the starvation that is occurring, the suffering that is being experienced, are the direct results of humanity, not God. It's humankind that seems determined to hurt and oppress people, not God."

"Okay." Scott interrupted McDonald. "But why does your 'God' just stand by and let it go on?"

"That's another good question."

Scott was starting to show some irritation with his adversary's politeness.

McDonald's training as a lawyer began to surface.

"First of all, if we're honest, we'd have to admit that, if God decided to get rid of all the people who hurt other people, he'd have to get rid of all of us as well." McDonald made a gesture that indicated the audience and more.

Wil was not overly impressed.

"Second, and more importantly, God didn't 'just stand by and let it go on.' That's the point. God didn't stand aloof and outside of this pain and suffering we cause each other. He entered into it in the person of Jesus Christ. He endured the beatings, mockery, and torture. He even endured the agony of death on a cross for crimes of which he was not guilty. Instead of remaining untouched by the agony we cause each other, he experienced it by choice. The reality is, God is better able to understand the suffering of those people in Cambodia than any of us in this room."

"But what good did it do?" inserted Scott. "The way I see it, your Jesus is dead and people keep dying."

"You're right," McDonald admitted. "But that's not the end of the story. God has said that one day the suffering will end and he will make all things right. The Bible says God accomplished this through His Son Jesus Christ."

"A lot of good that does the poor guy in Cambodia." Scott didn't seem convinced.

McDonald nodded. "But what I'm saying makes sense only if Jesus was who he said he was. That's why the resurrection is so important."

He looked kindly at Scott. "I can't fully answer your question. I can only say that I'm also trying to make sense of it all. I'm merely thankful we have a God who chose to become one of us and who knows how we humans feel, live, and die, rather than a God who doesn't care." He looked directly at Scott. "But let me ask you a question. Why is it that people blame God for suffering?"

McDonald didn't intend for Scott to answer the question, which was a relief to Scott. Asking questions is usually easier than answering.

"We seem to overlook that suffering and death result from human sin and activity, not God's desire for us." McDonald went on, "God desires wholeness and life. Whereas, humans, using one of the most precious gifts God has given us – *free will* – seem to desire something else. Perhaps if God took away our ability to choose, then suffering would – could – end. However, God desires to be in relationship with us." McDonald looked at Scott and asked another question he didn't expect Scott to answer. "But what good is a relationship if only one of the partners can choose?" He paused. "Without choice by both parties, you have something akin to slavery."

Scott was stirring, waiting to make his next move.

McDonald continued. "I wonder which is a bigger question, 'Why does God allow suffering?' or 'Why does God tolerate us at all?' The irony to me is that God's tolerance of humankind's activity and suffering is, perhaps, an even greater act of mercy." McDonald realized he was sounding preachy but was determined to finish his line of reasoning.

"God addressed humankind's negative choices and sin through His Son's sacrificial and substitutionary death on the cross. Through Christ, there is now a way to be free from the ultimate suffering event – death. We can be killed, but because of Christ, we do not have to die. In essence, God has conquered suffering and death by trumping it with eternal life – the gift He bought with His own blood." McDonald concluded, "If our lives are more than the 80 to 100 years we spend on this planet, then temporal suffering, while horrible, is in fact only a short-term issue. Beyond that, I will have to wait until I die to get more answers."

Wil was paying slight attention up to this point. However, his head snapped up at the next statement, a statement that fueled the fire now burning within him.

"But it is the evidence of the resurrection, the empty tomb, that brings it all into focus. If the resurrection did not happen, then what I have just said – in fact *all* of Christianity – is futile and meaningless. But the bones of Jesus are not there – the tomb is empty."

Unprepared for McDonald's last point, Scott made a mistake Wil had never seen him make before. He let the speaker turn and take a question from another person in the audience.

The big fish had gotten away. Scott looked like a person left without a chair when the music stopped. What else was there to do but wait for the next game? He sat down, not visibly convinced or moved by McDonald's answers.

"Let's go," said Scott, not waiting for Wil's response. They slipped out the side door with a few others. As they walked back to their dorm, Scott continued to bemoan his tactical error. How could he have let the opportunity slip?

Wil, on the other hand, could hardly believe the treasure he had been given. Jesus' bones! He would find Jesus' bones. Undaunted by the magnitude of his plan, Wil became consumed with this desire.

Back in his room, he wrote a letter to Steve, telling him he was going to become an archaeologist and discover the bones of Jesus.

From that point on Wil's determination to find the bones, to disprove the resurrection, to crush his dad's religion, overshadowed everything.

Throughout his academic and professional career, Wil was obsessed with this ambition. Harboring this purpose had been difficult. But he did. His obsession drove him through graduate school, away from Hope, through twenty-hour days, through death threats for trespassing, and through his balancing act of academic research and personal vendetta.

He had worked hard, become an expert, and positioned himself in Jerusalem with the Institute, all to carry out his objective. Few, other than Hope, Steve, and his mom, knew what drove him. The Institute knew nothing of it. His past professors and even his current colleagues could only guess at what drove him. To them he was a great archaeologist with the passion of a zealot.

Wil had become the world's foremost expert on historical sites in Palestine, specifically Jerusalem. His years of research and volumes of writings on first-century Palestine had won him prizes and grants and speaking opportunities. Now he had been selected to be on an advance security team because of his extensive knowledge of the area, and he could not believe the incredible personal opportunity this offered: the anticipated act of terrorists had opened the door for him to advance his quest. He would be looking for bombs in the very place he wanted to look for the bones. The collaboration between the U.S. and Israeli governments gave him access to areas his peer archaeologists only dreamed of. The unexpected opportunity was perfect. He felt closer to his goal than ever before.

Twenty-four hours earlier a car bomb in an Israeli settlement had killed one American along with the Palestinian suicide bomber and an Israeli tour guide. With the Secretary of State's visit only ten days away now, security was tightened. Wil's dialogue with local police units and the Israeli secret police had intensified. The haystack was too big, there wasn't enough time for their search, and they weren't even sure when their adversaries were going to hide the needle. But the team had to move ahead.

A status meeting was called. Colonel Rabin was at the whiteboard in the conference room recapping the criteria the team was using to identify the possible staging areas. He wrote:

1) The staging site(s) will be in or near Jerusalem,
in close proximity to the Temple Mount.

He was merely restating the consensus of the team, that the terrorists would attack close to where the Secretary's meeting was scheduled to be held. He didn't need to remind the team that the meeting was being held near the Mount for symbolic and political purposes.

Rabin continued writing:

> 2) *The attack will occur in an area of significant importance to Christians, particularly tourists.*

The terrorists called these pilgrims "Christian Zionists." According to the two experts on the team, these particular terrorists referred to all Americans as "Christian Zionists" and hated them perhaps even more than the "Jewish Occupiers."

The third and final conclusion the team had reached was next. He wrote:

> 3) *The attack will occur in an area not heavily populated by Muslims.*

This was the easiest deduction for the team. The terrorists had little reason to harm their own constituency.

The colonel relinquished the briefing to Steele as she started to speak, not bothering to ask her co-leader if he was finished. "There are a number of places fitting this criteria. The problem is we don't have enough time to search them all. Our best chance is to identify the most likely sites and thoroughly evaluate them. After talking with Dr. Wilson, I believe two sites are clearly the most suspect." Though the team had discussed these issues countless times before, this meeting felt like a final strategy session before D-Day. Steele and Rabin were determined to make sure everyone was on the same page. Steele continued. "Dr. Wilson, will you tell us about these two sites?"

Wil walked to the front of the room and turned to face the group. "The two sites are the Garden Tomb and the Church of the Holy Sepulchre." He identified them on a large map of Jerusalem. "Both are supposed sites of Jesus' burial. If the terrorists want to strike the 'Christian Zionists,' there could not be a better place."

Wil sounded like an encyclopedia. "The Church of the Holy Sepulchre is the site believed by most Christians to be the burial place of their Christ. It wasn't until the 1800s, with the discovery of the Garden Tomb, that there was a significant rival for its place of prominence. The arguments in favor of both sites are strong enough that most adherents to the resurrection of Jesus visit both places." He paused and added with a smile, "Just to make sure they cover all their bases."

Wil continued in his professorial approach. "The main historical problem with both sites is that of time and legend. It was not uncommon for a site to hold legitimate and special meaning for many, many years. However, the problem of accurately identifying these sites is compounded by the numerous foreign conquests, wars, and crusades that have taken place in this area. During such times, details were often forgotten or overlaid with a new legend. Periods of historical silence also served as a breeding ground for new myths and legends. While there was usually a historical reason for the reverence of a site, the exact specifics of what was believed a few centuries before was often overshadowed by the current legend." Wil caught Steele's look and realized he'd better conclude his academic tangent.

Wil knew all the details of the legend. Jesus of Nazareth had claimed to be God. The Jewish leadership rejected Jesus' ridiculous claim and accused him of blasphemy. According to Jewish law, anyone who claimed to be God had to be put to death. However, the Jewish leadership didn't have the legal authority to carry out capital punishment. Eventually the Jewish leaders convinced the Roman governor Pontius Pilate that Jesus was guilty of sedition, based on their assertion that Jesus claimed to be "*The King of the Jews.*"

The Romans took Jesus, after a series of beatings, to a place called Calvary and crucified him on a cross between two criminals. One of the criminals was reported to have converted to the belief in Jesus as Messiah, the Son of God, even as he hung on his cross next to Jesus. Jesus supposedly told the dying criminal that he would "be with me in paradise." Because of the torture Jesus suffered during and after his trial he died sooner than the other two men. According to the story, this meant that the soldiers did not break Jesus' knees. The other two men didn't escape this. Breaking the knees was the way the Romans hastened the rate of suffocation and death. All three received the traditional spear in the side, the Romans' final way to ensure their objective of death was accomplished. A wealthy, sympathizing Jewish leader named Joseph of Arimathea received permission to put Jesus' body in an unused family tomb.

One problem remained. Jesus had claimed he would rise on the third day after his death to prove he was the Son of God. Because of this, the Romans and the Jewish leaders were determined to not give Jesus' followers any opportunity to steal his body and create a substantially larger problem. Roman guards were placed in front of the tomb to ensure this did not happen.

This was merely history to Wil. He didn't have any problem with believing any part of the story since it all made an incredible amount of sense to him after his years of study of first-century Palestine. Where Wil broke rank with the Christians was with the myth of the resurrection. This legend began when, on the third day following Jesus' crucifixion, his followers claimed Jesus had been raised from the dead. The myth spread until today Christians around the world believe Jesus did rise from the dead. They assert that the resurrection proves his identity and his claims. To Wil, the myth was preposterous and he was determined to show it was misguided by finding Jesus' bones. He knew that if he could find those bones or somehow prove that Jesus did not rise from the dead, he would put a knife in the heart of Christianity and the religion his mother had hidden behind as his father beat him and her.

But this was not the team's issue, it was his. Coming back to the present, he said, "However, the details of the legend are not relevant to our current task. What is relevant is that, because of the tremendous religious significance attributed to these two sites, there has been relatively little archaeological work done at these locations, primarily because of the millions of tourists who visit these sites on a regular basis. It is also material that the terrorists know that very few of those tourists are Muslim."

Wil reached for a stack of papers on the table and began to hand them out. "These are detailed drawings and diagrams of each location. Also included are maps of their surrounding areas."

Wil answered a few questions regarding the papers he had handed out. Sarah Shner, the Director of Tourism, confirmed Wil's statements on the popularity of these sites. The experts on terrorism nodded in concurrence that these were the most logical choices.

After a brief silence, Steele stood. "So, are we in agreement that the two most likely sites for the terrorists to stage their attack are the two legendary tombs of Jesus?" Everyone nodded.

Wil was pleased and silently elated.

Truth can be denied, hidden, or misunderstood. It cannot be changed

Chapter 12

THE FIND

"We know you are looking." Steele read the terrorists' note to the team. Along with mocking the team, the terrorists were taking credit for the recent truck bomb explosion. They referred to it as "a taste of what is to come."

The Secretary's visit was now thirty hours away. The most difficult part of the team's work was keeping everything quiet. This didn't seem right. Nobody else, not the potential victims, not the regular police, not the tourist site operators, no one, except a small group beyond Wil's team, knew what the team was doing. It was ironic to Wil that, in trying to avert a major disaster and the deaths of a number of innocent tourists, the team had to politely maneuver around those same tourists to avoid a sense of panic. He wondered what those pilgrims would think if they knew that they were standing next to a pile of dynamite intended for fellow tourists less than two days from now.

The team had been assured that if they were unable to find the explosives prior to the Secretary's visit, the Israeli government would close all the major tourist sites for the duration of the visit as a way to minimize collateral casualties, but such a closure would be a desperate last resort.

Wil had never fully grasped just how sacred the tourism revenue was to the Israeli government. His understanding deepened as he sat through numerous meetings and observed the authorities' reluctance to do the logical thing – openly and aggressively search all the sites. Thinking of all the olivewood carvings, tiny bottles of water from the Jordan River, jars of holy land soil, T-shirts, toys, and tourist-trap bangles that sold by the truckload, Wil understood their reason. He concluded that Israel was one up on Disneyland. Israel didn't need an appeal cultivated by Madison Avenue.

Both probable attack sites were heavily visited, which made it very difficult for the team to conduct any serious investigation without attracting attention. It was particularly touchy at the Garden Tomb site since the group that owned and managed the area was a British non-profit organization. Following the tomb's discovery in the late nineteenth century, the Garden Tomb Association purchased the land and built a substantial wall around the area. Since the site was not directly under the authority of the Israelis, searching for the explosives was difficult.

The plan was that, on the night before the Secretary's visit, the Garden Tomb and the Church of the Holy Sepulchre would be closed down early "for maintenance." Through the American Embassy's influence with the British government, the British ambassador had persuaded the Garden Tomb Association to permit this "Israeli security effort."

Wil was to assemble two teams of three people, dressed as groundskeepers, to conduct a focused search of the two areas. Each team would include one explosives expert with a dog. If they were unsuccessful in their efforts to discover any explosives, the Israeli government would announce, late that night, the closure of all tourist attractions in and around Jerusalem. The head of the Tourism Department had made arrangements to set up a staging area with more buses than Wil dreamed existed. The government would provide free tours for disappointed tourists to other parts of Israel during the visit of the Secretary.

In short, the fallback plan was to thwart the terrorists' efforts to kill tourists by ensuring there would be no tourists to kill.

As for the Secretary, security would be seamless and, if they hadn't found the explosives, the meeting would be moved to an area away from Jerusalem. By removing the tourists and the Secretary, the two prime targets, the authorities hoped the terrorists would lose heart, make a mistake, and expose their cover. Wil was also directed to plan for some additional digs at other places if efforts at these two sites were unsuccessful. It was a good strategy and their only plan.

Wil was to lead the team at the Garden Tomb. He had drafted Dr. Ibriham Moshen, a noted archaeologist from Hebrew University and a close friend of Wil's, to lead the team at the Church of the Holy Sepulchre. Colonel Rabin was to be the liaison between the teams. Steele would remain at the team's base to coordinate if anything new came up. Everything was set. They would slip in, do some intensive searching, and be out in a few hours, hopefully having discovered and removed the explosives, all before the sites opened in the morning and everything continued as normal.

Wil told his secretary, Beth, that in the last few months he had moved from being a fuddy-duddy archaeologist to a respected scientist, to a security professional. He had now attained the rank of strike-force archaeologist. He wondered how that would look on his dossier.

With only sixteen hours left, they implemented their plan. It didn't take Wil long to get inside the tomb in spite of the fact that the British Garden Tomb Association's security guards had not been circumspect about their feelings. They were put out that they were not allowed to accompany Wil and his team. Unfortunately, one of the guards caught a glimpse of the uniformed Israeli soldiers who were supposed to go unnoticed as they sat in a van in the parking lot – *just in case*. This made the guards even more suspicious. They also could not help but notice the metal-detector-type devices each team member was carrying – and the dog. The guards resented being kept in the dark, since it was obvious that something big was going on.

Once inside the tomb Wil forgot about everything else. It was dark. The small window above and to the right of the door barely admitted a dusty beam of light. He let his eyes adjust to the dimness, then set up two electric lanterns, one in the antechamber and the other on a ledge inside the main chamber. His two assistants and the dog were patrolling the garden area outside and testing the firmness of the rock walls on either side of the tomb. Perhaps something was buried in the garden area. Wil was aware of the dog barking a few times, but thought nothing of it.

It was immediately obvious that no recent digging had occurred in the relatively small area inside the tomb. Wil's seeming calm betrayed the excited beating of his heart. He had been inside the tomb a number of times before, especially within the last two weeks. This was the first time without a swarm of tourists.

He remembered the first time he took the step down into the antechamber, turned right, and entered the main tomb area. He remembered seeing the three ledges where bodies were intended to lie. One was more "finished" and, according to legend, was the one on which Jesus' body had been laid. Wil wondered what the previous owner of the tomb would think about the fuss being made over this grave if, in fact, it wasn't Jesus' tomb. Wil had always hoped it wasn't. The tomb was obviously empty and, if it were Jesus' tomb, the empty tomb meant finding Jesus' bones would be even more difficult, if not impossible.

Wil spun around when he heard the commotion at the

entrance. His assistant, Ishmael, was coming into the ante-chamber with his hands in the air, the barrel of a handgun pushed into his back.

The gunman was screaming at him. "You shut up. Shut up! Or I give you same thing I do to friend."

Where on earth had this guy come from? How had he gotten past the Israeli soldiers in the parking lot and the security guards at the gate? Although, at this point, that really didn't matter. Wil was frozen where he stood. Where could he go? What could he do?

"Now sit or I kill you all," said the spindly, unkempt man, who spoke in heavily accented English.

It was clear that Wil was to sit on the ground next to his assistant, who had just received a severe blow to the back of his neck with the butt of the gun. The gunman stood in the middle of the antechamber pointing the gun at Wil, who was in the tomb chamber. Wil crouched next to his dazed assistant, their backs to the wall, looking toward the exit, the crazed man between them and escape.

Wil noted the attachment on the end of the gun. He assumed it was a silencer. Perhaps that was why the dog had stopped barking.

"Six years God says to me 'Misha, guard this tomb.' And so I do. Six years!" The gunman's eyes were glazed and his words stabbed the air. "You think you can desecrate Lord's tomb?" He became more irrational. "I know what you do – you sons of Judas. You come to put curse on tomb. I show you what happens to people who dare to desecrate this holy place." The man was almost preaching as he yelled.

As Wil stared at the assailant, he recalled seeing him outside the Garden Tomb gate on the team's previous visits. He had been passing out religious tracts of some sort and making comments about the need to "keep these grounds holy." Had he killed Wil's other team member? What was he going to do? Surely he wouldn't kill them in his "Lord's tomb." The sweat on the gunman's brow, his unkempt appearance, the way he seemed to pause and think, as if he were trying to figure out what to do next, suggested he was by no means a professional. The dirt and markings on his clothes led Wil to conclude that he must have climbed over the wall, unnoticed by the guards. However, professional or not, this lunatic had a gun and Wil did not want him to use it.

"We will leave and never come back," said Wil out of instinct. "We won't say anything. We'll leave and tell others not to do what we have done." Wil was rattling off assurances and apologies, sounding like a repentant teenager assuring his parents he would never be home late again.

"Shut up, you – umphh."

The gunman, who had been standing with his back to the entrance of the tomb, collapsed forward as another man crashed into him with a waist tackle. The impact drove the gunman and tackler against the wall where Wil and his assistant were leaning.

Colonel Rabin!

As he fell, the gunman fired a shot that grazed Wil's arm and ricocheted around the chamber. He fired again, without aiming, back toward the entrance of the tomb. The whole episode lasted less than five seconds and concluded with the gunman crying on the ground, babbling Bible verses, quoting from what Wil took to be the Book of Revelation in the New Testament.

The brief scene kept replaying in Wil's head as he straightened up, wincing in pain. He was puzzled by the disparity between the sound of the first shot, which grazed his arm and then ricocheted around the tomb, and the second shot, which seemed to make no sound at all other than a slight thud.

As he tended to Wil's arm, the colonel explained that the

other team had found a stash of explosives in a house next to the Church of the Holy Sepulchre. He had come to inform Wil. As he made his way through the garden toward the tomb, some distance from the gate, he saw the dog, limp and lying on its side. As he took a step toward it, he noticed the explosives expert, on his hands and knees, leaning against the wall of the garden. He had sustained a major blow to the back of his head and, having just regained consciousness, was able to tell the colonel what had happened. They proceeded to the tomb and saw the back of the gunman, in clear view through the tomb's opening.

Wil kept thinking about the gunshots.

"Your arm will be fine. Just a slight nick. I will get you to the hospital to get it cleaned up."

Wil stood up and apprehensively stepped toward the entrance of the tomb, ignoring the colonel's diagnosis. Rabin shifted his attention to Ishmael to see if he was okay, while also ensuring that the subdued attacker stayed put. Wil's hand extended toward a hole in the wall of the antechamber. The wall was opposite the chamber with the three ledges.

"This must be where the bullet hit," Wil mumbled to himself. "But where is the bullet?"

He leaned forward to take a closer look. Putting his finger into the hole, he scraped a little of the wall away. To his surprise the wall wasn't solid rock as it appeared and was thought to be. It was a mortar substance that was made to look, or perhaps over time had come to look, like the other walls in the tomb area. Was the bullet buried in the wall? He began to remove some of the loose material around the hole.

By now the colonel had noticed Wil's activity. "What are you *doing?*" The politically sensitive colonel was not at ease with Wil's defacing the wall of the antechamber.

Wil didn't hear him. He was too focused on the hole.

61

"Dr. Wilson. What are you doing?" The tone carried more than a request that Wil stop.

"The second bullet is in this hole. It appears this wall might not be solid."

The colonel approached Wil. Rabin was interested for two reasons. First, he needed to get the bullet. Not only was it evidence, but it would raise too many questions if someone else discovered it. Second, this might lead to another stash of explosives. Wil continued to scrape away at the hole, hoping the colonel's silence was also his consent. Reluctantly, it was.

The hole got bigger. Still no bullet. By now about half of Wil's hand fit into the hole. Then his fingers felt the bullet. It wouldn't move. With one of the tools he had brought with him he began to scrape away the material that held the bullet in place until, finally, he was able to dislodge it. The hole was now about five inches wide and four inches deep. The colonel gave the bullet a cursory examination. Wil didn't care about the bullet but continued to scrape the material out of the hole. He shone a flashlight into it. The back wall of the hole was a brick, more accurately, a flat adobe-type block. A wall!

He had scraped away the mortar covering of a brick wall. What was this? Adrenaline coursed though him. Why did he feel so much anxiety and panic? Maybe he was afraid the colonel was going to order him to stop. Perhaps this was why he did what he did – something no modern archaeologist would even think of doing. He reached for a pick ax and, to everyone's astonishment, including his own, without giving anyone time to question him or to object, gave one full swing of the ax with all of his might directly at the back of the hole.

Thud.

It was silent. Wil pulled the pick out and began to scrape away the new debris before sticking his hand into the hole.

There was no longer a back to his hole. Gasping, Wil pulled his hand out as if he had touched something hot.

He leaned forward again.

By this time the colonel, the two assistants, and the Bible-quoting maniac had grown silent as they watched Wil meticulously remove a little more of the wall, piece by piece. What was it? The colonel continued to hold himself in check. This would certainly be perceived by the Garden Tomb Association as a violation of the terms of their agreement. An understatement. But Rabin's feelings of obligation gave way to anticipation. Something unusual was happening.

Soon, with the help of a flashlight, they were looking through an eight-inch hole into another chamber area. They could see a skeleton lying on a ledge similar to those in the supposed tomb of Jesus. Wil studied the scene inside the new chamber.

"*The . . .*" Wil muttered. He adjusted his position so more light from his flashlight could reach into the black interior. Had it not been for the need to shine the light into the hole, Wil might have been able to fit his head in. He was reading something on the floor of the tomb, below the ledge with the bones. He was struggling to read it, not because it was written in first-century Aramaic, but because of the coat of dust that had settled.

"*King . . .*" Wil muttered more to himself than to the others, whom he had forgotten were there. The clarity of his words indicated he had no doubt regarding what he was deciphering.

"*Of . . .*" Silence. He blinked the dust out of his eyes and refocused.

"*The . . .*"

Wil stepped back. Beads of sweat were running down his ashen face. His breath came in short gasps. The colonel wasn't sure if he was in shock or pain.

"What?" asked the colonel.

As if to verify what he had just seen, Wil leaned forward and looked in the hole again. He read out loud in a definitive manner, "*The King of the Jews.*" Wil took a breath. "That's what the inscription says on the tablet lying below the body."

Wil pointed the flashlight so the others could see. It was as clear as if it were engraved on a tombstone in a local cemetery, except that it was written in first-century Aramaic.

Wil repeated into stunned silence, "The inscription says, '*The King of the Jews*'."

Chapter 13

THE PROJECT

When the awe of their discovery wore off and they began to talk to one another, it wasn't obvious what they should do. They were all convinced they had found Jesus. It seemed obvious, unbelievable as it was.

The colonel thought he'd better inform Steele. He dialed her on the cell phone. "Kathreen, this is Rabin." He paused. He was not too sure how this was going to sound. "We found something."

"More explosives?"

"Uh . . . well, no."

"What then?" barked Steele. She hated surprises and something told her this would be one.

"It is a long story . . . but I believe . . . that we have found the bones . . ." He cleared his throat, ". . .the bones of Jesus."

The phone was silent. Perhaps she hadn't heard him.

"We found the bones of Jesus," he repeated, intently.

Still silence.

"Kathreen?"

"Jesus? Like in the 'Son of God' Jesus?"

"Yes." The Jewish colonel overlooked the "Son of God" qualifier, knowing it was a statement of reference, not belief.

"Are you sure?"

"As sure as we can be. There is even a tablet identifying the body as '*The King of the Jews*'."

"What's Wilson think?"

"He's pretty certain, though he wants to do more research."
The colonel waited for a response. When there wasn't one he
said, "What do –"

"Hold it, Colonel! I'm thinking."

Her voice was clear and she sounded upset. This caught him
a little off guard. The colonel had already grown to dislike
Steele, and her tone only deepened his disdain.

"Don't do anything. I'm going to make a few calls. I'll get
back to you in fifteen minutes." She hung up before he could
respond.

The colonel took the phone from his ear and looked at it as
if it were a rude child. He turned to Wil and his assistants. "We
need to hold tight for fifteen minutes while Kathreen talks to
some people."

Back at the team base, Kathreen Steele took a deep breath.
The potential political repercussions crashing through her mind
were astronomical. She recalled her days in parochial school
when the resurrection of Jesus was taught as one of the most
sacred tenets of Christianity. These bones would certainly upset
that belief! Rehearsing what she was going to say, she picked
up the phone and pushed a few buttons. The President's secretary answered. Before the secretary could speak, Steele
demanded, "This is Kathreen Steele. I need to talk to the
President – NOW!"

"Yes, sir!" said the secretary.

Steele's tension was evident and her political wheels were
humming. She was extremely worried about how the surprise
discovery would play in the press – and the polls.

"Kathreen. What can I do for you? Did you find more
explosives?" The President sounded irritated with the disrup-

tion. After being briefed on the discovery at the Church of the Holy Sepulchre, he thought the situation was resolved.

"Sir, we have a problem."

"Take care of it."

"It isn't that simple, Mr. President."

Pause.

"What do you have, Kate?"

"Well, sir, it seems that while the other team was looking for explosives . . ." She paused and took another deep breath, hoping the President wouldn't think she was nuts. "Well, sir, it seems we've unearthed the bones of Jesus."

Both were silent.

"Are you sure?"

"I just received a call from the Garden Tomb, where the world's foremost archaeologist on first-century Palestine convinced an Israeli colonel that they have found Jesus' bones."

"They're sure?" The President did not want to believe it.

"Sure enough that we don't know what our next step is."

"Let me think."

Steele heard the intensity of the President, which usually preceded a statement of political genius. At such times his staff tried not to interrupt him by breathing too loud.

She added, "Sir, I probably don't need to tell you – the announcement of this discovery has the potential to alienate your Christian supporters and will not help your standing in the polls."

The President didn't respond. The enormity of the situation was obvious.

Steele waited. He was the President. She heard him speaking to someone else.

"Get me Prime Minister Aarons on the phone."

He must be talking to his secretary, Steele thought as she waited. She heard a click.

"Ehud?"

Steele was now on a three-way call with the Prime Minister of Israel and the President of the United States.

"How are you, my friend?" asked the Prime Minister. He sounded sleepy, but Steele knew that, like most world leaders, he was accustomed to being awakened in order to be briefed on important developments.

"I'm fine, Ehud. Thank you. I need a favor." The President was going to get right to the point.

"What is it?" The Prime Minister was still surprised to hear from his friend whose support had made it possible for him to win the last Israeli election.

The President's voice was casual yet serious. "I have Kathreen Steele on the phone with us. She's been heading up the search teams with Colonel Rabin. It seems one of the teams has made an unexpected discovery."

"Where?" By now the Prime Minister had already been informed of the discovery of the explosives near the Church of the Holy Sepulchre. Certainly the President wasn't referring to this.

"The Garden Tomb."

"The Garden Tomb?" repeated the Prime Minister, surprised and concerned. Christian tourism was vital to Israel's economy and this was one of the major sites. Was it good news?

"I'll get right to the point. The team thinks they found the bones of Jesus."

Kathreen could hear the Prime Minister gasp and cough at the same time before calmly asking, "Are you sure?"

"Yes. But we need to do some more research."

"So . . . ?"

"We need to keep this quiet. I cannot afford for this to come out before the election."

"Oh?" The Prime Minister was playing the game. He was

well aware of the President's precarious position in the polls. He also saw an opportunity for Israel to get something out of this situation, which could easily become a disaster for his country.

The President skipped the game.

"Ehud, let us bring the research back to the States. You keep it quiet on your end. We'll share all information. We buy some time and come up with a plan that's mutually beneficial. Israel eventually gets whatever artifacts are recovered."

Silence. The Prime Minister wanted more.

"And of course, Senator Brown will be calling you later today to see how you are doing."

That was the ticket. Senator Brown was the head of the Foreign Relations Committee and was well known for his reputation of funneling large amounts of money through Appropriations to countries that were on good terms with the President.

"Agreed."

"Ehud, there's one more thing. I want Kathreen to take care of the details."

"Of course."

"Thank you, my friend."

The two talked more casually for a few minutes while Steele excused herself and hung up. She immediately called the colonel.

"Secure the tomb. Secure all evidence. The Prime Minister and the President want this development kept under wraps and buried until they can figure out what to do. Colonel, this is TOP PRIORITY."

"The Prime Minister?"

"I was just on the phone with the President and the Prime Minister." This piece of news completely amazed the colonel. "Nothing is to be made known about this until I say so."

The colonel, who understood orders, understood this one.

They hung up. The colonel turned to Wil and his assistants.

"No one is to know about this. I have orders from the Prime Minister to secure the site until we can figure out our next steps."

Colonel Rabin dispatched one of Wil's assistants, ordering him not to say anything to anybody, to get the lieutenant who was in the parking lot with the security personnel.

The colonel grabbed the subdued gunman, who was by now as passive as a sedated dental patient, led him to the front gate, and told him to sit on a bench. Rabin ripped off a piece of the man's shirt, which had been torn either in his climb over the wall or in the scuffle in the tomb, and used it as a gag. He looked straight into the prisoner's eyes. "If you move, I will shoot you." The colonel walked toward the security guards at the front gate.

Either because of the look on the colonel's face or his purposeful stride, the guards realized something was up. They stood in anticipation.

"I am hereby informing you, on the authority of the Israeli government, that this property is now under the control and protection of the State of Israel until such time as it can be safely restored to its owner."

"What?" exclaimed the senior guard.

"You heard me."

Lieutenant Samuel Zahav arrived with his eight men and Wil's assistant. The assistant headed back toward the tomb.

"Sir," said the lieutenant. He saluted the colonel and also greeted him in a manner that indicated a comradeship.

"Samuel, we have found something that requires me to secure these premises. I need you and your men to establish a perimeter and not allow anyone to come in or leave these grounds without my direct order. You have permission to use *whatever* force is required."

The lieutenant raised an eyebrow.

"I am sorry Samuel. I cannot tell you anything else. I expect to encounter a lot of flak for this decision and you will need to be in top form. I will be in contact with you soon after I have worked out some details with our authorities."

"Yes, sir!" Zahav snapped and immediately turned to his men and gave the order. He had worked for Colonel Rabin before; it was clear he respected his senior officer.

Colonel Rabin interrupted him.

"Samuel, have one of your men escort these men to their vehicles and instruct them to go home." He gestured to the infuriated security guards, who realized there was nothing they could do. They had been in Israel long enough to know that when a colonel in the secret police gives an order, it will be carried out. The colonel started again.

"One more thing," he leaned closer to Zahav. "Who is your most trusted man?"

Zahav flinched a little, not wanting to think the colonel would question any of his men. He shifted his position a little and responded matter-of-factly. "Sergeant Barak."

"Good. Call him over."

Barak arrived and saluted both officers.

"Come with me, Sergeant." Rabin turned and walked back into the compound, where the now-terrified gunman was lying on the bench with his knees drawn up under his chin. "I want you to take this man to Captain Meir at the station. I want him gagged until he is put into solitary confinement. I want no one to speak to him or to remove the gag until I give the direct order. Do you understand?"

"Yes, sir," said Barak as he again saluted the colonel.

The colonel headed back to Wil and his two assistants in the tomb as Sergeant Barak led the subdued gunman out of the garden compound.

Meanwhile, Wil, not wanting to go any further until he could get his instruments and do it properly, would not let anyone near the wall, not that anyone was trying. He simply kept shining his light through the hole into the exposed tomb to examine as much as he could from his limited perspective. He must have read the inscription fifty times.

"I have secured the grounds," Rabin announced. "Please come with me. There is some work we need to do before we go any further." This wasn't news to Wil. However, he was unsettled by the way the colonel had taken over. Rabin continued, "Needless to say, gentlemen, we need to keep this quiet."

Wil had his own reasons for wanting to keep the discovery secret. Mostly, he wanted to be the one to pursue the dig. This imposed secrecy would help avoid the chaos of a herd of other scholars, archaeologists, and religious fanatics showing up, wanting in on what was likely the most significant discovery in two thousand years.

They gathered their belongings and straightened up what they could. The shell-shocked discoverers were trying to restore the site to the way it was before the evening began. It was futile, though, because there was no way to conceal the eight-inch hole in the wall. Wil took one last look through it before they headed back to the team's base to figure out their next steps.

Once there, the impact of the discovery began to overwhelm them. They decided to go with a cover story that explosives had been found at the Garden Tomb, because they wanted to do the excavation quietly and secretly to avoid any complications and unwanted attention.

Steele promised Wil unlimited funds as long as he went along with the cover story. This was a little troublesome to Wil, but he was reassured that the cover-up was only for a short period and that they didn't have a choice since this was the decision of the higher authorities. He agreed. He wanted to get on with the dig.

It didn't take long to get permission to close off the site. The British government publicly protested the seizure of property belonging to a British group, though it was obvious to Wil's team that their objections were for press consumption only. Wil was at the meeting at the embassy the morning following the discovery. The U.S. ambassador received consent from the British ambassador to allow the Israeli and American team to pursue their work. They convinced the British government it was necessary because of security and terrorist-related issues. Wil felt uncomfortable when the representatives of the United States government and the Israeli secret police explained to the British ambassador that the explosives discovered were so extensive that the Israeli action was reasonable. Wil held his tongue. He figured this was the way diplomacy was done. Furthermore, he wasn't asked to speak.

The cover story was working. The press reported that explosives had been found at the Garden Tomb and that, to ensure the safety of foreign tourists, the site would be closed for at least two weeks while safety measures were implemented. To substantiate the story, the explosives found at the Church of the Holy Sepulchre were displayed as a sample of the items found at the Garden Tomb. Nothing was said about the bones or the discovery of explosives at the Church of the Holy Sepulchre.

The Secretary's visit came and went. The advance team of which Wil had been a part was disbanded with the heartfelt thanks of the ambassador, who, through it all, had never been told about the discovery of the bones. Only the colonel and his superiors, Wil and his two assistants, the fanatic gunman, Steele, and a few others knew about the discovery of the new chamber in the tomb.

Wil was now carrying out the most exciting dig of his life.

He was amazed at the way the ruse played out in the press and the finesse with which the Israeli secret police carried it off. Even more impressive to Wil were the resources made available to him by a whole army of secretive people as he planned the excavation at the Garden Tomb.

They decided a team should be sent into the tomb with the focused objective of retrieving the bones and anything else obvious. It was concluded that the best approach was to get as much as they could on this first round and wait until things settled down before returning to finish the dig. The recovered artifacts would be taken to the FBI forensics lab in the States, where they could be studied without worry of being discovered.

They planned to return to the tomb at some point in the future, but the last thing any of them wanted was for the press or the tourists to think something unusual was happening at the supposed site of Jesus' resurrection. The "explosives" cover-up would be effective only as long as people did not see archaeologists traipsing in and out of the tomb with buckets of artifacts.

The first "hit" was under cover of midnight. Wil was not quite sure why, but the State Department sent someone to videotape the whole dig. Getting all of the archaeological equipment, strike team members, and the camera into the tomb unnoticed was a challenge. But they managed.

The camera started to roll and Wil began, this time with gloves on and much more cautiously, to remove the mortar and debris covering the newly discovered wall. The new chamber was on the other side of the antechamber, almost exactly opposite the old area that was believed for so many years to be the burial chamber of Jesus.

As soon as he had cleared enough space, Wil gently squeezed through the opening. He found himself in a chamber that, courtesy of the camera lights, felt like a Vermeer painting.

He was amazed at its condition. In the center of the room stood a stone bench, or table. With the exception of the wall he had just come through and part of the wall and ceiling area to his left, which looked as though it had crumbled before the cave was closed off, the room looked like it had been set up a few days ago.

In front of him, on a ledge that had been carved out of the rock wall, was the body, partially draped in the remains of a muslin-like fabric, the remnant of the burial shroud. The cloth was worn and fragile, but in remarkably salvageable condition. On the ground below the body, inscribed in Aramaic on a twelve by four inch stone tablet with one rough edge, were the words, "*The King of the Jews.*"

Could it have been this easy? Had he really found the bones of Jesus?

The wide-angle lens camera was positioned such that, were it not for the number of people in the tomb occasionally walking in front of it, the whole chamber was visible in the frame. Wil, his assistants, Steele, and the young red-headed American staffer who had been brought along to help move the artifacts, were in the tomb. The colonel and a few others were in the antechamber or outside the tomb helping with the packaging and moving of the artifacts. There were almost too many people in the small space.

Wil did a quick assessment of the situation like a detective at a murder scene. His assistants took some material for carbon dating and put it in their cases. One of his assistants, a forensic anthropologist, conducted a quick assessment of the bones and the shroud, and took a number of photos. Then the team began to transfer the skeleton, careful not to damage the bones or the shroud, into a specialized container destined for the lab. Wil studied the ledge that had held the bones, then examined the table in the middle of the room. He now was holding the tablet and studying it in astonishment and disbelief.

He turned to speak to the red-headed helper who was in the corner of the tomb where the ceiling had collapsed. The helper was bent over with his back to Wil, apparently examining something.

"Hey, you over there," Wil called.

The young man straightened up and turned around as if he had been caught with his hand in the cookie jar, adjusting his jacket as he turned.

"Bring that box over here." Wil motioned to a container that looked to be tailor-made for the tablet. "After I put this in the box, I want you to set it in the antechamber with the others." Wil pointed at the containers his assistants had set down next to the wall. "Be very careful with this one."

The young man did as he was instructed.

The camera recorded everything. Wil looked around for any other obvious clues, knowing he wouldn't be back for a while. Time was flying and they only had a little of it left. The team had moved the body container into the antechamber and was preparing to leave the tomb. Wil hated the thought of leaving. There was so much more. But the team had accomplished what they had come to do.

Wil's curiosity was still running wild. He wondered what the young helper had been looking at near the collapsed part of the tomb. It was obvious to Wil that that section of the chamber had crumbled at some point before the tomb had been closed off. Something prompted him to go and move some of the rocks. Perhaps it was simply his instinct to dig or an archaeologist's hunch.

He shifted one of the larger stones. The surprise was breathtaking. He saw a foot with a deteriorated sandal still attached.

Wil gasped.

"Ishmael, come here! Quick!"

Ishmael stuck his head into the chamber, trying not to get in the way of the camera.

"What is it?"

"I think I found another body."

Without saying anything, Ishmael stepped over to where Wil was standing. The two were so stunned they could hardly breathe.

"Send Benjamin back to the lab and get another container. We're going to take this with us also."

By now, Steele and the colonel were back in the tomb, drawn back by the urgency of Wil's call to Ishmael.

"We have to leave now," commanded Steele, although her voice conveyed reluctance.

"We can't leave now," pleaded Wil to an already convinced Colonel Rabin. Steele nodded her permission to continue.

After regrouping, they gradually uncovered the second body, apparently buried alive when this corner of the chamber collapsed. A number of the bones were seriously damaged. The skull, which had been fractured during the collapse of the cave, was still in superb condition. The man's ring and some scraps of cloth were also remarkably well-preserved. It was too much for Wil to comprehend.

Who was this? What had happened?

Just then, the second container arrived.

Wil's primary focus was on extracting the two bodies in as pristine a condition as possible. He knew the real work would begin in the lab. They had recovered enough material to work on for a lifetime. Still, he hated leaving, for he knew he had only scratched the surface in his research of the tomb. He eagerly looked forward to coming back. However, it was time to go to the lab. The team secured the chamber and left.

For two thousand years Christians have believed that Jesus was resurrected, that his body did not decay, that he had beaten death. For two thousand years legend had it that Jesus, having been dead for three days, walked out of this tomb alive. Now, after two thousand years, they were carrying his bones out in a box.

The significance of it all overwhelmed Wil. The voices around him faded into the distance as his mind was filled with a kaleidoscope of thoughts from his childhood beatings to his unveiled future.

Wil's team boarded the chartered plane bound for the FBI forensics lab in the States, the containers secured in the cargo area. The Israeli authorities had finalized the arrangements with the United States. The initial research on the bones would be done in the U.S. The two governments agreed that disclosure of any information regarding the discovery would be considered a breach of diplomatic security, and thus "TOP SECRET" was stamped on everything Wil and his team did. Even the project's expenses were kept secret.

The plan was to come up with the facts and then decide what to do. Perhaps it was due to his exhaustion, his excitement, or how focused he was on his work, but Wil never honestly asked why the two governments insisted on such secrecy about this project. He didn't really care. He told his secretary, Beth, that he was in the States on a special assignment. She was a bit hurt by Wil's secrecy, but thought nothing more of it.

Unfortunately, the veil of secrecy can be maintained only if everyone is in on the same secret. There was one factor nobody had planned on. The religious fanatic, who attacked Wil in the tomb, got lost in the shuffle. He was mistakenly released after a few days. Disheveled and wild-eyed, he showed up in front of the Garden Tomb entry gate and began to explain, to those who would listen, that he and some others had found the bones of Jesus. The Israeli secret police quickly arrested him again.

In response to the few press inquires regarding the religious fanatic's claims, the Israeli and U.S. governments did the only thing they could do. They defended the cover-up – and lied.

Truth can liberate or destroy. Why?

Chapter 14

THE COVER-UP

Wil hated hypocrisy. He hated a cover-up of the truth more.

"What do you mean – it's classified?" Wil was furious. "I want to see what's in that envelope!"

"I'm sorry, sir, but – "

One of the increasing number of government "suits" who seemed to swarm through the lab on a regular basis stepped in front of the shaken rookie and excused him from the scene. The confused young man walked away.

"I'm sorry, Dr. Wilson. Joe is new here and he doesn't know who you are."

Wil noticed Joe look back with a tinge of bewilderment at the senior official's explanation. To Wil, the project was becoming a frustrating, bureaucratic nightmare.

"Here's the envelope. I'm sorry for any inconvenience."

Wil opened the package to find a staffing plan for the project. No big surprise, though he had no idea who most of the people were or what they did. It didn't matter. He knew most of the core scientists, and his research was going ahead. Besides, there were so many names on the list that it was obvious they couldn't all be related to his project. The list was on White House letterhead, which was curious since it was the FBI lab and he thought most of the workers were FBI employees. However, nearly everything was beginning to seem peculiar on this project. Mundane things like stationery and staffing memos were unimportant to Wil when compared to what he was really concerned about.

Wil put the memo back into the envelope, having only glanced at it. He had received top-secret clearance from day one of this project. Nobody was going to hide anything from him. However, recently he had been encountering, mostly in whispers and innuendo, apparent efforts to cut him out of the loop. It was disconcerting. In this case, he was satisfied that he had not been denied access. His fury subsided for the moment and he handed the envelope back.

"Let me know if you ever have any other problems, sir. Again, I apologize." The suit turned and walked away, envelope in hand.

Wil noticed that he went into Dennis Brock's office. Brock was still an unknown to Wil, but it was obvious that he was the bureaucrats' head guy. His initials were at the bottom of most memos, and routing slips almost always started and ended in his office. In addition to Brock, more and more new faces seemed to be showing up each day. Everybody knew Wil, but Wil had given up on keeping track of them.

He'd been on some big projects before, but he had never worked with so many government types. The lab was better than any he had ever seen. The resources were endless. But the bureaucracy was stifling. As each day passed, Wil felt he was losing more and more control of the project. This disturbed his sleep.

Wil had gone along with the initial cover story about terrorist explosives in the Garden Tomb. There was a shred of truth to it. It was also intended to only be short term. He even believed the cover story would result in a greater good, namely the full exposure of the truth about Jesus without too much non-scientific interference. But, two weeks after the bones were discovered, it was becoming apparent to Wil that the truth might not be allowed to come out because of the President's concern about the discovery's impact on the election. Someone had jokingly floated this idea at one of Wil's staff meetings a week earlier. The man's superior quickly put the conversation back on track. The joker was reassigned elsewhere.

Unnerving.

Wil's team of experts and scientists had formally concluded that these bones belonged to none other than Jesus of Nazareth. The evidence was more than compelling – the carbon dating, the fact that the person had been crucified, the tablet, the shroud, the body of Joseph of Arimathea. (The other body was concluded to be, based on the jewelry and the location of the tomb, Joseph of Arimathea. According to the biblical account, Joseph owned the tomb where Jesus was buried). All this, plus more, combined to make the case for the bones being Jesus' overwhelming. Wil was increasingly concerned, though, that the bureaucratic power structure might keep his discovery under wraps for much longer than he thought he could bear.

Various government officials had told him privately that they were withholding the announcement until the right time. It was becoming increasingly clear to Wil that the right time might never come. Why would they reveal the discovery of the bones after the election, since this would expose their pre-election, politically motivated cover-up? Plus, by then the bureaucrats would have so infested the project that Wil knew he would have lost control of the discovery. Wil had moved from doubting their sincerity to rejecting their words outright.

And then he heard some disturbing news from Israel. The Garden Tomb had been determined to be permanently unsafe. No one had been in the tomb since Wil's team had retrieved the remains of Jesus and Joseph of Arimathea. Now no further access to the tomb would be allowed. Ever. Next, he heard that the religious fanatic from the tomb was mysteriously found dead. When Wil could not get a consistent answer about what had happened to the gunman, his thoughts began to border on paranoia.

After Wil heard the project's spokesperson, who was tightly connected to the President, feed a new lie to the press, explaining why Wil was in the FBI lab, Wil knew things were getting out of control.

He had found the bones of Jesus.

No one would ever know.

He not only hated the thought of his discovery getting buried, he was beginning to feel as if his realized dream of refuting Christianity was slowly slipping out of his hands.

Chapter 15

E-MAIL TO STEVE

To: Steve (PastorSteve@DC.net)
From: Wil (account7269@InternetCafe.com)
Subject: CONFIDENTIAL
Date: June 24, 1999

I AM WRITING FROM AN INTERNET CAFE. I AM CON-CERNED THAT MY PHONE AND E-MAIL ARE BEING MONITORED. PLEASE DO NOT CONTACT ME REGARD-ING THIS!!!!

Steve, tomorrow is a big day. The reason you haven't heard from me for a while is that I have been incredibly busy with my work. I have made a discovery that I am certain will send shock waves throughout the world. It is so important that no one, outside of a few people in the State Department, the FBI, and the Israeli government, is even aware of it. The President is concerned about the repercussions of my discovery.

The reason I am writing you now is that tomorrow I am going to do something dramatic. The material I have discovered is likely to be buried again, but this time in a mountain of bureaucracy and political considerations. Well, you know me, I hate that stuff.

What I am going to announce tomorrow is so important that I will not let it be buried again. Watch the news tomorrow night. CNN. I will be in D.C.

Wil

Chapter 16

E-MAIL FOR MOM

To: MikeWilson@Columbia.net
From: Wil (account7269@InternetCafe.com)
Subject: CONFIDENTIAL – WATCH THE NEWS
Date: June 24, 1999

Mike:

I AM WRITING FROM AN INTERNET CAFE. I AM CON-
CERNED THAT MY PHONE AND E-MAIL ARE BEING
MONITORED. DO NOT CONTACT ME OR TELL ANYONE
ABOUT THIS E-MAIL!!!!

This is important Mike. Get Mom and watch the news tomorrow night. CNN. Dad was wrong.

Wil

Truth is unavoidable.

How you respond is your only choice.

Chapter 17

THE ANNOUNCEMENT

Betty and Mike Wilson sat in front of the television in Betty's home. "He said to watch the news. I'm sure it will be on sometime." Betty Wilson spoke in an optimistic but hesitant tone.

"Do you have it on CNN?" barked Mike, who had settled in for the entertainment of seeing his little brother on TV.

Betty nodded. The CNN logo was displayed in bold on the bottom right hand corner of the screen.

"Hold it!" Mike sat up straight and put out his hand toward his mom as if to silence her, even though she wasn't talking. "I think this might be it!"

The television screen showed an anchorman in front of a background graphic of a cave with yellow police tape across the entrance. Above the cave were the words "Jesus' Bones Found."

"We take you now to Washington, D.C.," said the anchorman, "where CNN's correspondent, Connie Johnson, is standing by to report on an announcement made by world-renowned archaeological historian, Dr. William Wilson. The announcement has caused tremors throughout archaeological and religious circles. Connie."

"Thanks, Charlie." The camera showed the pretty, blonde reporter outside a busy conference room in what looked like a posh hotel.

"Today at four o'clock p.m. Dr. William Wilson, world-renowned archaeologist, announced he had discovered the bones of Jesus in what could best be described as a previously undetected chamber in the Garden Tomb of Jesus, outside Jerusalem."

The screen now showed a recording of the press conference at which Wil had made the announcement.

"There he is," exclaimed Betty.

"Be quiet," shushed Mike, who was by now staring at the TV and listening as if he had heard that aliens had landed in New York City. "Be quiet, I said!" Mike repeated in a louder, more intense voice, though Betty already sat subdued. "Didn't you hear what they said?" Though not a Christian, he understood the impact of this news.

The film clip started with Wil standing at a podium in front of a number of reporters. He fidgeted with the knot of his tie and ran his hands through his hair. Clearing his throat, he began:

"Three weeks ago we made an amazing discovery. It happened while I was on a project for the State Department in cooperation with the Israeli secret police. In anticipation of the Secretary of State's visit to Israel, we were looking in likely places terrorists might be using to stage an attack on the Secretary. As part of that process, we began to evaluate some of the popular tourist sites. Among the places where we looked was the Garden Tomb, which had been speculated to belong to Joseph of Arimathea and to be the burial site for Jesus of Nazareth, the central figure in the Christian religion.

"While there, I happened to notice something in the wall of the antechamber of the tomb. It was interesting enough that we received clearance to do more archaeological assessment. After going through about seven inches of mortar, brick, and dirt, we hit dead space – a pocket.

"Upon clearing the debris we discovered an extension of the tomb, which apparently had been closed off following a collapse of the ceiling and a part of the wall nearly two thousand years ago. Upon entering the chamber, we discovered two skeletons in remarkably good condition. We also found, next to one of the bodies, a stone tablet with the Aramaic inscription, '*The King of the Jews.*' "

Wil paused and took a deep breath. You could see the perspiration on his brow.

"Upon further investigation, we determined that the younger remains were those of a Hebrew man in his mid-thirties who died by crucifixion around 30 A.D. Clear markings on the bones above his hands and through his feet indicate spikes had been driven through them in accordance with the Roman method of execution by crucifixion. The shroud revealed that he had been severely beaten prior to his crucifixion. Forensic anthropologists have concluded that one of the man's knees had been broken, likely while he hung from a cross, and that he died of suffocation. A lower rib bone with a groove etched into it gave evidence of a spear having pierced his side.

"The second set of remains is believed to be those of Joseph of Arimathea, the owner of the tomb where Jesus was buried. This other man had a fractured skull, which resulted from the collapse of the chamber's entrance that closed the area off for nearly two thousand years.

"It is now obvious that the empty chamber, the one called the Garden Tomb, which shares the same antechamber as the one where we found the two bodies, had been mistakenly assumed to be the tomb of Jesus. We believe the absence of a body in the empty chamber became the basis for the legend of the resurrection of Jesus.

"Based on the evidence, which includes carbon dating of

the bones, forensic work by the most skilled experts in the world, analysis of miscellaneous artifacts, and other irrefutable evidence, we have concluded that what we have found are indeed the bones of Jesus of Nazareth."

Wil paused as if preparing to answer questions. The picture moved from the press conference back to a split screen format with half of the screen showing Connie and the other half showing the anchorman.

"Connie," the anchorman began. "From the reports we are getting here, it seems this discovery has caused quite an uproar in Christian theological circles. In fact, the news of the discovery has sent shock waves from Harvard to Dallas Theological Seminary, from the Vatican to local Christian churches everywhere."

"It sure has, Charlie," agreed Connie. "The discovery of the bones of Jesus, whom Christians call 'the Christ,' strikes at the very heart of one of Christianity's most fundamental doctrines, namely the resurrection of Jesus."

"How so?" queried Charlie in a leading fashion.

"Christians believe that Jesus rose from the dead on the third day after his crucifixion. That's why they celebrate Easter. The resurrection is believed to be the final and conclusive proof that Jesus was the Son of God.

"The reason Christians are so concerned is that if these *are* the bones of Jesus, then Jesus did not rise from the dead as has been believed for nearly two thousand years. It would be like finding out George Washington really was not our first President, that the world really is flat, or that we never really landed on the moon."

"My guess is we have not heard the end of this story. Thank you, Connie."

The screen returned to normal and focused on the anchorman.

"And now, let's go to Tokyo where the President is meeting

with other world leaders at the World Economic Summit to discuss trade . . ."

The TV volume seemed to disappear.

Betty was crying. Mike was staring at the air in front of him.

Few things are as absolute

as relativism defending itself.

Chapter 18

THE SPIN

It took the White House spin doctors less than twenty-four hours to put together their plan and explanation. They had hoped to avoid addressing the reporters regarding Wil's announcement until after the President had returned from the World Economic Summit in Tokyo. They were not that fortunate, but they were prepared.

The leaders of the most powerful countries in the world stepped onto the stage of the Tokyo Hilton. Although they had just negotiated the most comprehensive trade agreement in a decade, it was as if none of what they had been working on mattered.

The first question came from a reporter with the *Los Angeles Times*.

"This question is for anyone who would like to address it," began the reporter. "Did you discuss the situation regarding the bones of Jesus recently discovered in Jerusalem?"

It was an awkward moment, but the leaders all seemed prepared as they deferred to the U.S. President, who quite obviously had been designated to field this anticipated question. Wil, watching the situation unfold on the TV in his D.C. hotel room, thought he saw frustration or anger on the faces of some of the men behind the President. This was particularly true of the British Prime Minister, who had by now realized the deception to which the British had been subjected from the time the bones were first discovered.

The President stepped closer to the microphone. "Yes, we did." His candor caught the room of reporters by surprise. They were all convinced the President had been caught in another cover-up and that they would have to work their way through the weeks of spinning and hedging before they could get a straight answer. However, the election was only months away and the President's campaign managers had decided that the only way to avoid this situation blowing up in the President's face was to take control of it.

"Yes, we did," repeated the President in a definitive, reassuring, and solemn manner. "However, before I discuss the issue, I want to thank Dr. Wilson for his diligent work and for his willingness to articulate the significance of the find so effectively. His willingness to explain the matter while I was tied up in these trade talks was appreciated and helpful. A person of his stature is always welcome when dealing with issues such as these."

Wil, who rarely watched the news, did a double take. What did he just hear?

The President continued. "As Dr. Wilson explained, the world has in fact found the bones of Jesus of Nazareth. And, as my friend Dr. Wilson alluded, this find is not only of significance archaeologically, it is also of significance historically, and specifically, in the area of religion. Knowing the bones would cause great concern to Christians around the world, I decided it would be best if, before we went public with the news, we were absolutely sure that what had been discovered were, in fact, the bones of Jesus.

"Having been convinced beyond doubt that these are the very bones, I personally made the decision to review the issue with the leaders represented here as well as with other national and religious leaders, including the Pope, with whom I have recently been in contact. I fully supported Dr. Wilson's making the announcement.

"In addition, I have personally appointed a special committee of religious leaders and elected officials who, with the support of other world leaders, will study and evaluate the impact this discovery will have on religious and social issues. I have asked my friend and trusted public servant, Senator Harold Brown from Massachusetts, to chair this committee, which he has graciously agreed to do as a service to his country."

This blatant plug for Senator Brown surprised some. The pundits picked up on the obvious electoral impact immediately. They would talk about it on the evening talk shows, asking each other what impact Brown's appointment would have in the tight senatorial race between Brown and Congressman Henry Newcastle. This race had drawn national attention. Newcastle was running as an independent in what had become a neck-and-neck race between two candidates formerly of the same party. Brown had his party's backing and the President's support. Newcastle, who had taken what he called a temporary sabbatical from the party in order to unseat Brown, had significant grassroots support.

After a brief pause, the President began again in a tone that implied everyone understood the impact of the recent find.

"As you know, I too have called myself a Christian. And now, knowing that Jesus really did not rise from the dead and that his claims to be God are not substantiated, I, with my family, have had to deal with the impact this has had on our religious worldview and life. I am in the same boat as so many others who have believed for their whole lives what has just been proven to be a falsehood." He paused, looking grieved.

"However, I am committed to moving forward into whatever new age or challenging worldview this new chapter brings. My hope . . ." The President again paused, swallowed, and looked straight into the camera, talking directly to the TV audience, ". . . is that my country will afford me the opportunity to lead them into this new, *Post-Christian Age*."

The President stopped and looked at the crowded pressroom as if begging them to move on to another subject. "Please understand that, at this point, this is all we are prepared to say about this subject. I have scheduled a special press conference when I get back to Washington to address the whole issue in much greater detail. We have a lot of other matters to discuss and, on behalf of the other leaders, I am requesting that we move on to these other issues of significance."

The miracle was that the press granted the President the courtesy he requested.

Wil turned off the TV. He could hardly believe what he had heard. He had never formally met the President. The President's national security advisor had specifically told Wil's team that the President absolutely wanted to keep everything top secret. He had been certain, prior to what he had just heard, that his announcement would gain the President's wrath, not his praise. Regardless, Wil knew now that the President had staked out his position for the pending election. He was going to turn Wil's find into a steamroller and ride it back into the White House.

Wil could only wonder what he had done. Fully clothed, he lay on the bed for about thirty minutes, eyes wide open, hands behind his head, taut with anxiety. He had gotten himself into a quandary and he wasn't sure how it was going to end. He clicked the TV on again to find something to get his mind off the predicament he was beginning to realize was not going to go away. Unfortunately, he could not avoid it.

As the TV screen brightened and the picture came into

focus, Wil found himself looking at two figures sitting at a semi-circular desk facing each other.

Royal Lawrence, the host, was looking into the camera. "I'm here with Keith McDonald, famous lecturer on college campuses, renowned apologist for Christianity, and author of numerous books, including *The Resurrection Reality* and *A Case for Jesus*." Lawrence shifted his focus to his guest. "Keith, thank you for being here."

Wil could hardly believe it. Twice in less than twenty-four hours! He hadn't heard Keith McDonald's name since the night his roommate had dragged him to the Student Union Building hoping to have a great debate with this man. And today he'd encountered him twice. Earlier that day he received a call, out of the blue, from McDonald. They talked for about fifteen minutes. Now he was seeing him on TV. Wil thought McDonald looked tired and a lot older. He also looked sad.

"So what was the first thing you did when you heard the news about 'The Bones'?" asked Lawrence.

"I was going to go to Israel to see for myself," said McDonald.

"Did you go?"

"No. I found out it would be pointless. It seems that, following the announcement, there have been numerous threats of terrorist activity against the site. The Israeli government has cordoned off the area. They are also still concerned about the explosives they found a few weeks ago."

"Had you been to the site before?"

"Yes, as part of my research, before I wrote my book *The Resurrection Reality*."

"That's the book in which you argue in favor of Christianity based on your research and investigation as a lawyer – and as an atheist, I might add?"

"Yes, that's the book. However, I wasn't arguing in favor of the Christian religion per se. I was arguing that Jesus was the unique Son of God," McDonald elaborated.

"What do you mean by 'not arguing in favor of the Christian religion'?"

"I believe that what matters is not the adherence to a set of religious concepts. Surely they are important. But what really matters is that people have a relationship with God through Jesus Christ. That was the point. For thousands of years we humans have been trying to structure our lives so that we might approach God or please God. In Jesus we have God coming to us. By Jesus' paying for our sins on the cross, Christ made it possible for us to be restored to a relationship with God. The point of my book was not to convince someone about a religion. It was to convince people that Jesus is who he said he was and that he alone is the way to have a relationship with God and inherit eternal life."

"Hmm . . ." Lawrence was a little upset that McDonald had gotten slightly too preachy for his show. "What did you do after you decided not to go to Israel?"

"I have an acquaintance, a pastor, who has been a long time friend of Dr. Wilson's. He said he hadn't been able to reach Dr. Wilson since the announcement but suggested I try to call him anyway. I was fortunate enough to get through to Dr. Wilson, who told me about his work and what they had discovered."

Wil was still regretting that he hadn't shown more discretion and kept his mouth shut until the dust settled. But McDonald had caught him at a weak time and when McDonald said he knew Steve . . .

"What did you find out?"

"Too much," responded McDonald. "That's the problem."

"How so?"

"I was convinced by the overwhelming amount of evidence

that they might be right. Yet, I hoped that this was a hoax or a mistake or mere speculation. I would then have had a reason to fight on. The evidence these experts have put together is pretty compelling – the bones, the artifacts, the carbon dating, the location, and most of all, the engraved tablet. However, I still have some reservations."

"Has Dr. Wilson's find caused you to question your faith?"

For the first time McDonald looked reticent. Until then, he appeared more objective, more comfortable, more removed. After that question, he sat back, sighed, and seemed to think about his answers more than he had previously. "I wouldn't put it quite that way, but it does present a number of challenges."

"In what way?"

"If they are the bones of Jesus," McDonald paused. "I mean if they *really* are the bones of Jesus, that means Jesus did not rise from the dead, and the resurrection did not happen. That would be devastating to me and all Christendom. I have argued for years that if the resurrection did not happen, then Jesus was a fraud and we who call ourselves Christians are to be pitied."

"That seems awfully strong," commented Lawrence.

"It is meant to be. You see, Jesus of Nazareth claimed to be the Son of God – God incarnate. He is recorded as doing miracles and being a great teacher. He fulfilled many Old Testament prophecies related to the Messiah. However, when he was asked what sign or proof he would give to substantiate his claims about himself – that he was the Son of God – he responded that he would rise from the dead in three days. People didn't quite get it at first. Rise from the dead? Who was he kidding? But for almost two thousand years, we who call ourselves Christians have believed he did precisely that. In fact, I would have to say that if there is one historical event on which the entire validity of the Christian faith rests, it is the resurrection. If those bones are the bones of Jesus, he never rose from the dead and we have been duped."

"Duped?"

"I have spent my adult life arguing in favor of the resurrection and the divinity of Jesus Christ. This discovery challenges the fundamentals of my faith. If they are the bones of Jesus, it will not threaten my faith, it will kill it."

"Kill? That's another strong word."

"I know. But if Christianity is anything, it has to be based on truth. It must be based on fact. And until now, I was convinced it was. If the resurrection didn't happen, Jesus is not who he said he was. He said he was God. If he were not resurrected, he would be just a dead liar or a dead lunatic. I could not be a follower of a madman. Sure, Jesus had some good things to say. So did Mohammed and Buddha. Even some major atheists and dictators have had some good things to say. But great words are not enough to make a man worthy of worship. I believed Jesus was different. Without the resurrection, he is merely another man."

"You use the word 'if' a lot," noted Lawrence. "Why?"

"The jury is still out, in my opinion, as to whether they are the bones of Jesus."

Lawrence looked amused and surprised. "You do realize you are in an extremely small minority don't you, Keith?"

"I've been told that." McDonald looked like a defeated man.

"But you're not convinced?" inquired Lawrence.

"One issue is that one of the knees of the man was broken."

"Oh?" Lawrence smiled. He had heard this objection before. "You must be referring to the contention based on the 'no broken bones' prophecy."

McDonald looked slightly offended. Lawrence was seeming to belittle something that Christians for two thousand years had held to be a fulfillment of prophecy. At the same time,

McDonald could not suppress his own doubts on the accuracy of the prophecy or anything he believed. The one broken knee was the last thing McDonald was holding onto before being forced by the overwhelming evidence to concede that the bones were the bones of Jesus. It was all he had. McDonald leaned forward and began.

"The Bible states that none of Jesus' bones were broken, unlike the two men who were crucified at the same time as Jesus. This fulfilled a messianic prophecy that no bones of the Messiah would be broken. In this prophecy Jesus is portrayed as the Passover Lamb whose blood protects and cleanses those who trust in God. None of the bones of the Passover Lamb were to be broken. Since Jesus was the new and eternal Passover Lamb, the prophecy means that none of Jesus' bones would be broken."

Lawrence brought the conversation out of the realm of theology to the pragmatic. "But Keith, isn't it possible the 'no broken bones' legend was put forth by the same people who concocted the resurrection story?"

McDonald leaned back in his chair and conceded, in what sounded more like a confession, "As a lawyer who is trained to consider other possibilities, I'd have to say yes." McDonald seemed to be resigning himself to the inevitable.

"And what about the engraved tablet?" Lawrence sounded more like a prosecuting attorney than a talk show host.

"I know," conceded McDonald. "The inscription, the body, the carbon dating, the other evidence, such as the fact that it is the tomb I personally thought was the most logical place. These have created a lot of concern for me."

"It is creating a lot of concern for a lot of other people too," added Lawrence. "Perhaps we will get more answers to these questions as time goes on."

"Yes," McDonald added, more to fill the void of silence than to add to the statement.

Lawrence turned to the camera. "Keith McDonald, author, lecturer, lawyer, theologian, seeker."

He turned back to McDonald. "Thank you for being with me tonight. It has been a pleasure."

"Thanks, Royal," responded McDonald in a courteous but lifeless voice.

Royal Lawrence turned again and looked directly into the camera. "Please join me tomorrow as we talk with Congressman Jerry Jones from South Carolina, the man behind the initiative for a congressional investigation surrounding 'The Bones' – what some are calling 'Bonesgate.' This week – as we continue our focus on 'The Bones of Jesus' controversy."

Wil turned off the television and decided he needed to get some sleep.

Chapter 19

KENNY

"Talk about a skeleton in your closet. The President said he just found the skeleton of Jesus in his!"

Kenny Reno was beginning his monologue.

Steve had hardly slept since Wil's announcement. As he sat watching the late-night talk show, he was thinking how peculiar it was that America's late-night talk show comedians were usually the first ones to truly go to the heart of the issues in the news. Did they get the same reports as their evening news counterparts? And how were they able to get their monologues and guests in such a timely manner? Who would have thought thirty years ago that a late-night comedy talk show would become a primary forum for the issues of the day?

"As you heard, they have found the bones of Jesus, and the President has asked that he be allowed to lead us into the – what did he call it – the 'Post-Christian Age.' The 'Post-Christian Age!' It sounds like something every teenage boy goes through. My question is: How did he come up with that term? Follow me . . .

"First, Jesus claimed to be the *Christ* (or Messiah) and that he would rise from the dead to prove he *was* the *Christ.*

"Second, Jesus didn't rise from the dead, so he obviously *wasn't* the *Christ.*

"Third, therefore, how can we have a 'Post-*Christ*ian Age' if Jesus wasn't the *Christ* in the first place?

"Am I the only one who thinks these things through?

"And what about property values?" Reno hit his stride. He pulled a copy of the *New York Times* from his back pocket. "Just a second. I saw it earlier this morning. . . . Here it is." Reno began to read. "'Pope Considering Options.'" He glanced up like a teacher ensuring her class was paying attention and then began again.

"'A Vatican spokesman acknowledged today that Catholic scholars were allowed to look at the evidence in the FBI laboratory. The only comment made officially was, 'It is disturbing.' However, an inside source has informed the *Times* that high-level conversations are occurring related to the vast worldwide property holdings of the Roman Catholic Church. The source said that the bones discovery will likely cause membership and donations to diminish, requiring the disposition of some of its holdings.'"

Reno looked up from the paper, letting it fall to his side in one hand. "Do you realize what would happen if the Catholic church started to sell its property? We're talking about colleges, parks, monasteries, hospitals, churches, cemeteries, houses. We're talking major real estate! If they dumped all of that on the market . . . Jeez – what a mess!"

Reno's attention was directed offstage. A guy with a headset and clipboard walked on stage and handed him a note. He read it to himself as the stagehand exited. It was obvious Reno had been thrown a curve ball, and when he looked up, he appeared perturbed. He did not like being told what to do.

"Well, I've just learned one thing. My bosses actually watch the show!" The audience laughed. "I've been instructed to read this disclaimer." He held a three- by five-inch card in front of him as if he were announcing the winner of the Oscar for Best Actor. He read, "It is not the policy of this station or any of its affiliates to formally comment on the real estate market. Any opinions of its employees are only opinions and should be considered as such."

Reno put the note in his pocket, sighing with overemphasis. "I feel better now." He looked pleased. "I've heard that they had these notes ready to go, but this is the first time I've ever been carded." Reno grinned in a way that revealed inner pleasure. This brought out another laugh from the studio audience as he added, "Do you think I hit a chord?"

Reno resumed his monologue. "On a similar note, this thing has caused quite the uproar on Wall Street as well. Apparently, people are concerned that Christmas spending is going to go down. The Christmas season makes up a large share of so many retailers' sales. This is a *big* concern. I understand the Federal Reserve is even trying to figure out what this means related to inflation and interest rates. I can hear it now. 'If Jesus didn't rise, does that mean interest rates should fall?'

"But not to worry! Earlier today, I was informed that they've decided to go all the way and drop the *Christ* out of *Christ*mas. Santa is in big time! The plan is to go all out for Santa. Rather than *Christ*mas, it's going to be called *Santa*season. Everybody loves Santa and, since he hasn't ever died, no one is concerned about digging up any bones.

"They are going to have to work on some of the songs though. I've already come up with a couple. Rather than *Away in a Manger,* we could sing *Away in a Ford Ranger.* This one should be a real favorite for hunters who, deep down inside, are always disappointed they can't shoot the reindeer – have you ever noticed the racks Rudolph and his buddies are carrying?

And, rather than *Joy to the world, the Lord is come*, we could have *Joy to the world, my paycheck comes*." Reno let the laughter ebb.

"If you have any other ideas, I would like you to write them down and send them to me. I realize it might be premature, but I figure we need to get these things written and learned before the season comes and we have to listen to *Frosty the Snowman* all Santaseason long.

"Did you hear about the hubbub that came up at the United Nations today? It seems some of the Islamic and Hindu nations have made a formal request of the United States and other 'Christian nations' to get their Christian missionaries out of their countries. It also seems one of the results of this discovery is that some of the other religions are seeing an opportunity for proselytizing. After all, nearly one-third of the earth's population has been identified as Christian. Now that we are in the 'Post-Christian Age,' it seems that there is a scramble to fill the void. I actually heard that some enterprising Muslims, Hindus and Buddhists are trying to recruit some of the Christian tele-vangelists to their cause. I can hear it now, 'Buddha wants you to send in your money.' Or, 'Let's all sing a round of *Mohammed loves me, this I know, for the Koran tells me so.*'

"Did you hear Congressman Jones of South Carolina today on CSPAN? There is actually a call for congressional hearings on the discovery of these two thousand-year-old bones. They are calling it – get this – 'Bonesgate.' My suggestion is that those congressmen all grab one of those bones and start whacking some sense into each other. Bonesgate? What are they going to think of next? Each time I hear of a new 'gate,' whether it's Filegate, Whitewatergate, Chinagate, Newtgate, or Irangate, I wonder what would have happened if Nixon and his boys had broken into the Hilton. It simply wouldn't have worked! Would it be 'Fileshilton' or 'Iranton or 'Newthil'? They simply don't have the same ring, do they?

"The weirdest thing I've heard so far, though, was what my

nephew said. He got really upset and said, 'Mohammed*@%!'
When I asked him why he said 'Mohammed*@%!' he told me,
in the matter-of-fact way that only a sophisticated seven-year-
old tough guy can, that it wasn't cool anymore to cuss using
Jesus' name. I can see it now. The next time I hit my finger with
a hammer, I'm going to have to say 'Buddha*@%!'

"Thank you . . . thank you! Hey . . . we have some great
guests tonight. Please join me in welcoming . . ."

Steve had had enough. Not only were his wounds deepened
by Kenny Reno's levity concerning the decimation of his faith,
he really didn't care what Julia Roberts or Britney Spears had
to say about the state of the world and their lives. He turned off
the TV and headed up to his bedroom, where he had hoped to
find his wonderful wife getting some sleep. He was disappointed to see the light on as he quietly opened the bedroom door.
Wendy got out of the bed to comfort him, even though she too
was hurting.

"We'll get through this, Steve. We only need some rest and
some time."

The king's men stood, having successfully put Humpty-Dumpty back together. But was it Humpty-Dumpty?

Chapter 20

THE CHURCH

The congregation sat in silence as the young but seasoned pastor stepped to the pulpit of First Church of Hazel Dell. Pastor Wally had been at the church for eleven years. He had come to the church at its lowest point, after the previous pastor had skipped town with his secretary. When the congregation had asked the deacons' council how it was possible for the pastor and his secretary to have had an affair for more than seven years without any of them knowing, they learned that most of the deacons were also being unfaithful to their wives.

To complicate matters, the treasurer, the pastor, and a few of the other deacons, including one who happened to be the police chief, had developed a creative embezzlement scheme that had left the church near bankruptcy. Though the discovery of a few white robes and some Aryan literature got the most play in the newspaper, the situation was, in reality, much worse.

The congregation had been decimated. Two-thirds of the members left. A completely new deacons' council was elected. Pastor Wally was hired directly from seminary. He served as pastor, youth director, music director, custodian, and receptionist for about two years before the congregation began to grow.

And it had grown. The church was now healthy. It had a sizable and active membership, and was involved in the community, ministering to victims of alcohol abuse, and supporting overseas missions. The members loved their pastor. Everything was going fantastically.

And then Wil Wilson, the adult son of long-time church member Betty Wilson, announced he had found the bones of Jesus. People had thought it couldn't get worse than it was eleven years ago. But it did. This news that Jesus had not risen from the dead made the earlier trouble seem like child's play.

Pastor Wally's eyes were puffy and red. He wiped away the tears, trying to appear less broken. The experiences of the past eleven years made him look much older than his thirty-eight years. The experiences of the past few days made him look ill. Wally found it peculiar that this emergency church meeting, which had been announced only twenty-four hours ago, had more people in attendance than any service he had conducted during his pastorate. Even more than Christmas or Easter. But there were no hymns. There were no candles. No robes. No choir. Not even a sermon topic.

Wally tapped the microphone. He had never done that before. Perhaps it was a nervous gesture or a symptom of his feeling completely inadequate and totally unprepared for what was about to happen. He looked at the group. The church was packed. There wasn't even any room in the aisles. The children had all been left at home. The fire marshal's sign above the door declaring the maximum capacity didn't apply tonight. Except for an occasional sniffle, the church was silent. All eyes were fixed on him. Would he start with a joke? He had done that at many other times when things were tense, in order to break the ice. He didn't have a joke.

"First of all, I want to apologize to those of you who have been trying to get in touch with me before tonight's meeting. I had to take some time to think. I'll be back in the office tomorrow morning if you want to see me." That was the easy part.

Wally shook his head, trying to clear away the mustiness that enveloped him. "I don't know what to say . . ." By the look on his face, it was true.

"All of you have seen the announcement and the talk shows and the news. How could you avoid them? I've been doing my level best to try to make sense of it all. It's been hard, as I'm sure it has been for all of you. I've talked with my friends at the seminaries and in government. I've looked at this thing in every way I know how. I – " Wally stopped to regain his composure.

He began again. "Some of you have expressed reservations about the bones being Jesus' because one of the man's knees had been broken. I've also seen this discussed on the news – most of you probably have also. This objection is based on a passage from the New Testament, John chapter 19, which reads: 'The soldiers therefore came and broke the legs of the first man who had been crucified with Jesus, and then those of the other. But when they came to Jesus and found that he was already dead, they did not break his legs.'

"I must admit I also noted this discrepancy with the body they found. Since one of his legs was broken, I resolved it couldn't be Jesus. I've tried to hold onto this, looking to it as a lifeboat of hope in an overwhelming sea of darkness. However, I have to be honest with myself. This is only one small prophecy. There is so much more to consider. After reflecting on all that was found, it doesn't seem wise to base one's faith exclusively on these few words. Such a position would be nothing more than wishful thinking.

"Many of you have asked me what I think. Many of you asked me point blank if they are the bones of Jesus or not." Wally had come to hate that question. But it would not go away.

"I have to tell you," he started over, "I've been asked many questions in my lifetime. None of them has been as troubling as this one. I certainly have never been so concerned with the accuracy of my answer. I'm well aware that my answer will affect many of you. I wish it weren't so, but I know it is. When it comes down to it, all I can really say is that we all have to make up our own minds. We should consider the evidence, make a decision and move forward. I want all of you to know that each of you has much to offer each other and – "

"*ARE THEY JESUS' BONES?*" A man in the middle of the church was standing and looking directly at Wally. Wally knew him. He was one of his strongest supporters. However, the force of his question, interrupting Wally's attempt to be pastoral in the face of a crisis, left little doubt that all of that was now immaterial. There was no malice in the question, only a sincere desire to know.

Wally knew he had to answer the question. He took a deep breath, put his hands on either side of the pulpit to brace himself.

"I believe they are."

Silence.

It was as if the buzzer of the championship game had rung just as the final shot rolled around the rim three times before popping out. Many sighed in defeat. Most had their eyes cast down. And then people here and there began to cry. Not loudly, but weakly, as if a beloved spouse of sixty years had just died and left the other alone on this big planet, no one to share life with anymore.

Wally said again. "Yes – I do believe the bones they found are the bones of Jesus of Nazareth. I don't want to believe it," he lifted his hands palms up, "but the facts are what they are." A few people began to get up and slowly walk out of the church, their heads hanging low and their glazed eyes fixed on the floor in front of them. "But we cannot give up." He didn't sound convincing. "Just because Jesus was not who he said he was does not mean there isn't much we can learn from his teachings."

Even to himself these words did not sound reassuring. A few people shook their heads, still telling themselves, "It can't be." A few more got up to leave.

"Besides, we are a family and we have much to offer each other." Wally felt like a coach consoling the last-place finisher of the most important race of a lifetime. He remembered the helplessness he had felt after hearing that his wife had been diagnosed with metastatic lung cancer. He started to move his lips again but was not able to say anything. What more could he say?

"Why don't we all take some time to think about things? I'll be here all day tomorrow and will make myself available to any of you at any time. Good night." Tears welled in Wally's eyes. He grabbed the papers he had set on the pulpit but not referred to, and walked slowly through the silent sanctuary to the exit and then his car.

Wil's mother was sitting in a pew near the side of the church. Her life had finally come together after all of those unhealthy years with her abusive husband. Her faith was now hers. And then this. Her face was in her hands as she leaned forward over her knees. She was beyond tears. No one talked to her. They wouldn't have known what to say if they had tried.

Most of the questions
on life's test are known.
Why is so much time spent
trying to answer questions
that have not been assigned?

Chapter 21

THE HEARINGS

"Who was paying you while you were working on the project?" probed Congressman Jerry Jones, sitting with the rest of the congressmen in front of Wil. His southern accent was preamble to his brilliant mind and sharp wit.

"I was and remain an employee of the Institute of Palestinian Archaeological Research. I understood my work to be an extension of my role with the Institute."

"So you were paid by the Institute for your efforts on the project?"

"The issue never came up."

"What about your expenses?"

"I don't really know. I've always had my expenses reimbursed through the Institute."

The ultra-conservative congressman who had initially called for the hearings continued his line of questioning. "Once the bones were discovered, did anything change?"

"No."

"So, you were always paid for your time and research by the Institute?"

"I believe so."

"You are not aware that your personal expenses, including airfare, meals, phone calls, and deluxe accommodations – where you are still staying – have been paid for with taxpayer funds?"

"Truthfully, Congressman, I haven't thought much about it. I assumed the expenses and details would be worked out with the Institute." Wil was going to add that he didn't bother keeping track because Steele had told him he would have unlimited resources made available to him, but before he could say this he was interrupted.

"You assumed wrong," said the congressman. He began again with a different tack. "Is this Institute known for any specific religious orientation?" Wil was slightly indignant at the congressman's accusatory tone.

"Mr. Chairman!" exclaimed Congressman Newcastle from the other side of the panel. "May I remind the gentleman from South Carolina that this inquiry, which I feel to be a misguided waste of taxpayer funds, is not a court of law and that Dr. Wilson is not on trial. Nor is anyone or anything else for that matter!" The distinguished-appearing gentleman sounded uncharacteristically like a defense attorney in a rush to state his case to the jury before the judge could overrule his objection.

"The Chair asks that the congressman from Massachusetts wait his turn, which he will get. The congressman from South Carolina may continue." You could hear in the chairman's voice the sympathy he felt for Congressman Newcastle's objection as well as his slight irritation at Congressman Jones's approach, even though he was a member of his own party.

Congressman Jones started again without missing a beat. "As I was saying before the gentleman from Massachusetts interrupted me . . ." Jones paused and turned to the chairman. "Mr. Chairman, will you please add one minute to my time, which the gentleman from Massachusetts used up in his interruption?"

"Continue, Mr. Jones." The chairman sighed.

"So . . ." Jones turned back to Wil. "Is the Institute known for any specific religious orientation?"

"The Institute of Palestinian Archaeological Research is one of the finest academic and educational institutions in the world. In my area of study, the Institute is without a doubt the leader in the world. It approaches academic endeavors from an eclectic point of – "

Jones interrupted. "Please answer the question, Dr. Wilson."

"I am merely trying to state that at the Institute there are people of various philosophical viewpoints who – "

Jones interrupted again. "Dr. Wilson, please answer the question. Isn't it a fact that the Institute is predominately made up of atheistic, Jewish, and Muslim researchers with a minority representation of Christian academicians? Isn't it a fact that Christian approaches to history, particularly regarding early Christianity, are not welcome at the Institute?"

"Well, I – "

"And isn't it true that, in fact, the formal position of the Institute is that the New Testament record of the life of Jesus is understood to be a biased religious account recorded by a few extremist Messianic Jews?"

"There are some who hold to that perspective, but I don't understand what that has to do with anything."

"Nor do I," objected Congressman Newcastle. "Mr. Chairman, since this charade is apparently going to continue, please ask the gentleman from South Carolina to stick to the point at hand."

"Mr. Jones," said the white-haired chairman in the center of the panel. "While I agreed to conduct these hearings based on the evidence you presented to me, it is within my authority to bring this hearing to a close. However, out of a desire that nothing be hidden from the people of this great country, I will indulge you for a few more minutes. But please, stick to the point!"

The room was quiet. In fact, these hearings were rather

peculiar. They were called on short notice at the request of the congressman from South Carolina. When Congressman Jones was interviewed by Royal Lawrence, he asserted that the issue of Jesus' bones, while of religious significance, brought to light an important constitutional issue. He alleged that there was evidence of government activity in anti-Christian endeavors paid for secretly by the federal government in an illegal manner. The congressman claimed he had evidence that taxpayer funds and resources were spent on what was clearly an anti-Christian endeavor. Three days after Wil's announcement, and after a secret meeting in the chairman's office, the hearings were convened and Wil was summoned to Congress.

Congressman Jones resumed. "Dr. Wilson, once the bones were discovered, what was done with them?"

"We took them to the FBI forensics lab because of the sophistication of their research facilities."

"Was the FBI lab on contract with the Institute?"

"Not that I know of."

"Did you or the Institute or anyone ever pay or reimburse the FBI lab or the federal government for their time and expenses?"

"I don't know."

"At what point did it become clear that there were significant, and predominately religious, issues related to the bones?"

"After my team speculated that we had discovered the bones of Jesus."

"Was the United States government interested in the bones at that point?"

"I don't know," responded an exasperated Wil. "I was only interested in doing my research." Pausing, Wil thought about his answer a little more. "Perhaps they were. I know the Israeli government is interested because of the age and historical importance of the find. There have been some U.S. officials from the State Department involved throughout the whole project. Truthfully, I've never really known why. But again, I didn't really care."

"Dr. Wilson, why were the bones really sent to the FBI lab?" The congressman's tone was uncomfortably accusatory.

Wil shifted in his chair and leaned forward. "As I said, I was told it was due to the sophistication of the FBI research facilities. It all happened so fast. It was quite exciting. I was pleased to have access to such an exceptional research facility. Before I knew it, I was in the lab with a number of the top experts in the world as part of my project team." Wil was going to tell the congressman how an official from the White House had told him the entire resources of the lab would be available for his research and that the Israeli and American governments had struck a deal regarding the initial research taking place in the States. Again, the congressman spoke before Wil had the chance.

"Are there many Christians assigned to your project?"

"I don't really know or care. That has nothing to do with anything," responded Wil, again indignant.

"Are you a Christian?"

"No, but again that has nothing to do with anything," repeated Wil. He was irritated by the congressman's tone and was still uneasy about the direction the questioning was taking.

Seeing Congressman Newcastle preparing for another objection, Jones redirected his questions. "Do you have any idea about the cost of the investigation during the two weeks following your discovery?"

"No," admitted Wil again, visibly frustrated with the line of questioning.

"Well, for your information, I have before me an estimate of the costs of the project." Jones held up a piece of paper. "It includes staffing, equipment, your personal airfare, expenses,

FBI costs, scientific experiments, materials, etc., and was prepared by the Congressional Accounting Office. It states, may I read, 'It is estimated that at least 12.8 million dollars of taxpayer funds were expended during the first two and a half weeks of The Jesus Bones Project'."

Wil was speechless. Steele had promised unlimited resources, but he could not comprehend how his team could have spent nearly that much money. He was about to mention his surprise with the figure when the congressman sat up straighter and took a deep breath.

"Dr. Wilson, would you consider these bones to be an issue of national security?"

"No." His eyebrows rose.

"Of vital trade interest?"

"No."

"Related to the security of the President or any elected official?"

"No."

"Do you believe that the funds expended on your project were authorized by the Congress of the United States?"

"I don't know."

"Let me tell you, sir, they were not!"

Congressman Jones sat back and the room quieted. He began again, this time slowly and deliberately. Babe Ruth was pointing to left field and preparing to hit the ball over the fence for the boy in the hospital. "Would you say these bones are primarily of religious significance?"

Wil thought a little longer about this one. "Yes, though they also present some extremely interesting academic and archaeological issues for further study."

Ignoring the second part of Wil's response, the congressman continued, "Isn't it highly unusual for the government of the United States to be involved in matters of predominantly religious significance?" This question was for his fellow panelists and the cameras, not for Wil.

"Congressman Jones, you have one more minute. Please conclude your questioning," informed the chairman.

Jones pushed his chair back and stood. "Mr. Chairman, I would like to recap what we have heard." He sounded like a prosecutor making his summary comments to the jury.

"Over the last two and a half weeks, without the appropriate authorization of the United States Congress, 12.8 million dollars of hard-earned United States taxpayers' money has been spent on a project under the leadership of an employee of a foreign institution with blatantly anti-Christian positions in an investigation which, by the project director's own admission, is of predominantly religious significance and, I might add, anti-Christian in nature." He paused and took a deep breath. "What we have here is a fundamental and clear violation of the separation of church and state through illegal activity by the State Department and the FBI in their use of federal funds for an endeavor that is not within their scope of activity, nor one which Congress or the people of the United States have asked them to pursue!"

"That is ridiculous! Preposterous!" The congressman from Massachusetts was angry.

"Ridiculous?" retorted Jones. "Preposterous? What's preposterous is that what I've just said isn't obvious to the congressman from Massachusetts. Or perhaps it is, but the congressman is refusing to acknowledge it because it fits so nicely into the well-known, anti-Christian political agenda he has articulated for so many years. Perhaps he is even reveling that he has finally found a champion for his cause!" Congressman Jones was savoring this part of the battle.

The room began to resemble the floor of the stock exchange

during a major market correction. Lines were drawn. Accusations were flying. It appeared blows could happen.

"Gentleman! Order! Gentleman! Gentlemen! Order!" The chairman was pounding ferociously with his gavel. "This meeting is adjourned until tomorrow at ten a.m."

Wil could hardly believe his ears. He sat stunned. Never had he dreamed this would be the outcome of his work. Members of the United States Congress were battling with each other over a few million dollars spent on the most important archaeological find in history.

As he walked out of the room to the front steps of the Congressional Building, he was again reminded of the deep chord he had struck. From the top of the stairs he read signs with a variety of messages: "Wil Wilson, a Champion of Truth!" held by a man who seemed to be of Arab origin; "Stop Government Anti-Christian Activity!" carried by a man with a white clerical collar; and "Jesus Lives. The Bones are a Hoax!" held by someone amid a group of people singing hymns.

Wil felt alone. He wondered what he had really done. As he started down the stairs he felt a hand grip his arm. He turned.

"Hey, Wil, can I buy you a cup of coffee?"

"Steve!" Wil gratefully shook Steve's extended hand. "It's great to see a friendly face."

"My car's over here." Steve pulled the shell-shocked Wil in that direction.

Chapter 22

THE PRESIDENT

Wil's meeting with the President was unsettling. The President had been back in the States for a day. Wil had sat before the congressional hearing panel. Things were buzzing in the lab, and then he was summoned to the White House. He was very nervous. Cameras and reporters were everywhere. The President's smiles were plastic. It was hard to believe that people couldn't see that the spirit of joviality between Wil and the President was a sham, but Wil played along. He knew he had already caused enough consternation for the world's most powerful person, and it was apparent this was an important photo shoot. Wil didn't see any reason to make matters worse.

The press eventually retreated. The President, a few of his advisors, and Wil were now alone. The President gestured for Wil to take a seat at one of the chairs around a large, cherry-wood coffee table. Wil felt out of place, privileged, and suspicious. The three advisors were: the President's chief of staff, Dwight Jordan; the President's chief counsel, Greg Landes; and Roland Stein, who apparently did not have a title. When Kathreen Steele came into the room and joined them, Wil's stomach muscles tightened. He met her piercing gaze with as much steadiness as he could.

There was some stiff small talk. After the pause that followed, the President looked directly at Wil. The room was silent. The others were also staring at Wil as the President said, "Next time you decide to change the world, Dr. Wilson, let me know in advance."

Wil wondered if he was being scolded. Or was this a joke? He swallowed with difficulty.

"I want you to know, Dr. Wilson, how much we have all appreciated your hard work. What I want to know is – do you still want to work on this project?"

Wil's heart was pounding. "Yes, Mr. President. I do – very much." The President's question cut deeply. The desire to go back to the tomb and continue with the dig was burning within him. Was this another threat?

"That's good to hear. A person of your stature is valuable to us and to the world as this whole thing unfolds."

"Thank you," said Wil although, in his mind, he questioned the President's sincerity.

"Dr. Wilson – or may I call you Wil – we are standing on the brink of a new chapter in human history: an evolution of western civilization, if you will. You need to understand that I plan to lead the nation into this new 'Post-Christian Age'." Wil had come to hate that phrase. The President had embraced it.

"It is my understanding that you and Kathreen had a deal back in Israel. You broke that deal with your announcement. However, that is in the past. I want you to be a part of the team – *my* team." The President narrowed his eyes. His lips were smiling, but his relaxed posture belied the tension of a coiled snake. "But, Will, let me tell you straight out, I do *not* like surprises. And you surprised me the other day with your announcement."

Everyone was silent as if to let the President's words penetrate into Wil, who wasn't sure if he should run or laugh or breathe. The silence was broken when the President turned to Stein and said, "So how was your trip to California, Roland?"

They moved on to the weather, the schedule for the rest of the day, and then the little meeting ended. The President went back out to the press and, after one more photo where the President had his arm around Wil's shoulders, a White House staffer escorted Wil to a back door, thanked him for his time, and dismissed him. Wil stood on the outside stoop feeling soiled. A guard ushered him to a side gate. "Goodbye, Dr. Wilson." The gate closed. Feeling like a prisoner set free, Wil decided to head back to the lab.

The President retreated to his office with his three advisors and Steele.

"So what do you think?" asked the President.

"I think you made your point," said Stein, who seemed to agree with everything the President said.

"I'm still a little concerned, sir," said Chief Counsel Landes. "He could be a loose cannon. I know it appears that, after his announcement, he doesn't have any more big cannon balls to lob in our direction, but he seems a little too independent to me."

"What do you suggest?"

"Should we 'deal' with him?" asked Jordan. The chief of staff's words trumpeted his military background.

"Would you relax?" interjected Steele. "We've been on him, and I really don't expect there to be any more surprises as long as we keep him under wraps."

"That's what you said a few days ago, before his announcement," contributed Landes. The chief counsel was reported to be the President's most levelheaded advisor. He and Steele did not get along.

His comment stung. Steele had been more surprised than anyone by Wil's announcement. She had assigned Dennis Brock to the project five days before the announcement to keep

Wil in check. Brock had even put in place a number of obstacles intended to limit Wil's control and influence on the project. Brock and she were floored by Wil's unannounced press conference. Nevertheless, she really did believe any damage Wil could do was already done and there wasn't much to worry about. She ignored the comment and turned to the President.

"My suggestion is that we gradually phase him out and then deal with him when he's not the center of attention."

"Agreed."

Steele was pleased that her plan was so quickly approved. But it wasn't unusual for the President to make quick decisions, particularly when he had other things on his mind.

"How are the polls looking?" he asked.

Stein spoke first again. "Fine, sir. It looks like the election is going to be yours. The 'Post-Christian Age' platform is playing great."

"I know." The President was boasting. Stein and the President had been through many campaigns together. "I must admit I was a little concerned about how the Christian voters would respond to the news. But, thanks to Dr. Wilson and our stepping up to the plate, it seems things are going to turn out quite well." The two smiled at each other. They had done it again.

Stein continued, "The polls are showing that at least ninety percent of the people who used to call themselves Christians are now solidly in your corner. They're your key to another four years." He sounded smug, savoring the taste of victory.

The President's demeanor grew serious, but he was still smiling. "Let's keep it that way."

"I'm still very concerned about the congressional hearings," said Landes, bringing everyone back to the present.

"Me too," agreed Jordan.

"Explain." The President looked at Landes.

"Well, sir, we've been successful at keeping Congressman Jones focused on the separation-of-church-and-state issue. I was thrilled when they blew past the 12.8 million dollar figure in the hearings, thanks largely to the skills of our friends in the Congressional Accounting Office. It was a little too close for comfort, though. Sir, this turn of fortune might not last."

"You're worried about the payroll diversions." The President got right to his chief counsel's concern. He directed the next question to the group. "Any ideas?"

"Take the hit and move on," said the chief of staff.

"What do you mean?" asked the President.

"Let's confess that we did get a little too close to the line and that we shouldn't have funded the research. Let's agree with Jones that the church-and-state thing is at the heart of the issue. The way I see it, the people don't really care. We could submit to a slap on the wrist and close the books on the congressional hearings. We do not want Jones and his cronies spending too much time on this. The idiot might stumble onto the bigger issue – the payroll diversions to your campaign."

Stein spoke next, ignoring Jordan's comments. "How about going after the congressman and putting him on the defensive so he doesn't have time to focus on the money?"

The President nodded.

"Perhaps we should stop diverting funds to your campaign through The Bones Project," suggested Landes.

This suggestion was not acceptable to Stein. He stated his disagreement even as Jordan was preparing to second the motion. "We need those funds. Plus, Kathreen says she has everything under control." Steele appreciated the vote of confidence.

"Are you sure about that?" The counsel was yielding, but making it clear that it was his opinion that they were in treacherous waters and needed to be extremely careful.

Again ignoring the comment, Steele said, "How could Dr. Wilson ever find out? Dennis Brock is now screening the payroll and staffing records. Besides, I'm telling you, this guy is so focused on his research, I doubt he even cares about the election."

It was silent for a few moments as the President was processing. "Kathreen, this is twice in a few minutes I am going with your recommendation. Are you confident you can deal with this situation?"

Steele knew this was much more than a question. "Yes, sir!" Her tone of confidence was for her own sake as well. The chief counsel and chief of staff were not happy with the decision.

The President said, "Let's get back to work then." The meeting was over. As the advisors left the room, he asked them to wish him luck. "I'm off to that elementary school again for another photo shoot. I hate driving through that neighborhood, and those kids get on my nerves."

Chapter 23

ROYAL

"Welcome back. We have been talking about the 'Bonesgate Hearings' on Capitol Hill with Congressman Henry Newcastle of Massachusetts, who is running for the Senate against Senator Harold Brown, the President's hand-picked chair of the special committee studying the impact of The Jesus Bones discovery." Royal Lawrence returned from a commercial break, having just had the congressman articulate his concerns about the hearings.

"Joining me now are the Reverend Dr. Winston F. Buckingham, Reformed Episcopalian bishop and author of The *Myth of Jesus* and *A New Concept of God*; Rabbi Benjamin Goldstein, author of *Judaism for Today*; Jennifer Ishihara, director of the Buddhist Community of Faith in West Los Angeles; and Dr. Steve Halterman of Washington's First Church, D.C. Dr. Halterman happens to be a long-time friend of the archaeologist who discovered the bones of Jesus, and the pastor of the church attended by Congressman Jones, the driving force behind the congressional hearings.

"Let's start with you, Dr. Halterman," began Lawrence. "What has it been like for you since the discovery of 'The Jesus Bones'?"

"Naturally, Royal, it hasn't been easy. People in my congregation have responded in a number of different ways. A large number of them, after viewing the evidence, simply stopped coming to church. Others have come to me asking how to make sense of it all."

"And what do you say to them?"

"What can I say to them? This discovery is devastating. If Jesus did not rise from the dead, then he was not who he said he was, and we Christians have been living a lie, a myth, and – "

"Excuse me." Steve was interrupted by Reverend Buckingham, who ignored Lawrence and looked directly at Steve. "I have to ask this question. Why are you evangelical Christians getting so bent out of shape by this? As I stated in my book, the resurrection is only a 'religious-faith myth' in the first place. It was conceived by the early Christians as a way to give them hope, even though they knew it wasn't true. They passed on this hope through the generations and, after centuries of doctrinal development, the belief in an actual resurrection surpassed the hope-myth. Can't you see that?"

Royal Lawrence sat back. This kind of conflict did wonders for his ratings.

Steve didn't have time to respond.

"I agree," said the Buddhist Community director. "We in the Buddhist tradition recognize Jesus as a great, enlightened teacher. The discovery of the bones of Jesus does nothing to change our perspective about him. It was his message, his teachings, his understanding of the universe that made him great. For two thousand years the Christian Church . . ." Ishihara gave a nod to the bishop that indicated she wasn't implicating him, ". . . has misunderstood who Jesus really was. The bones do not matter. It is Jesus, the great teacher, who is to be revered, not this so-called God/man the Christian church created."

"But – " Steve could not get a word in. He was overshadowed by the volume and intensity of the other panel members as they argued that Jesus was a great and good man, not God, and that the resurrection didn't happen, nor was the resurrection even an issue of importance.

Steve felt as if he were being beaten. It wasn't that the other guests were expressing such fervor against him that made him feel isolated and vulnerable; it was the resonance of their words. Ever since the bones were discovered, Steve had done some serious soul searching. He remembered reading Keith McDonald's book in college. That book had helped him understand that Christianity was not a religion that required one to check one's mind at the door. He recalled learning of the concepts of grace and forgiveness and eternal life in a way that gave him hope and confidence. He remembered the countless arguments and discussions in the college dorm and at seminary, when he would articulate that the reality of the resurrection was the foundational historical event that validated Jesus' claims to be God and enabled Christ's death on the cross to make sense.

He also remembered his many conversations with Wil and how determined Wil was to find the bones of Jesus and prove that Christianity was a lie. Though Steve did not want to accept that the bones were Jesus', the evidence was compelling and devastating. The arguments of his current antagonists kept him up night after night as he re-evaluated his profession, his worldview – his whole life – in light of what his co-panelists were articulating.

"Please, madam and gentlemen." Calm settled across the panel as the elderly rabbi spoke softly into the tension. "Our friend, Dr. Halterman, is not the enemy. He has not even had a chance to express his ideas. How is it that you choose to focus all your comments at him? I, for one, can only have empathy for my brother who has obviously, with his flock, had to deal with a significant event in his faith journey. I, like my brother, am having to deal with this revelation.

"While we in the Jewish faith have never believed in the resurrection of Jesus, we have long believed that Jesus was a good man and a worthy teacher, a rabbi. We have also believed that the misunderstandings about Jesus have caused many of our Jewish brothers and sisters to follow this man as if he were the Messiah. This was only a misunderstanding. I see in this discovery the great opportunity for those who have long made up the Judeo-Christian worldview to break down this artificial barrier caused by this misunderstanding of Jesus and to once again come together as we strive to serve the God of creation."

The Rabbi's comments were so solemnly spoken that the other speakers, out of respect for the revered elder, did not want to break the silence his words had caused.

"So, Dr. Halterman, what do you think?" pressed Lawrence, knowing too much silence did not make for a good show.

Steve sighed. "Honestly, I feel somewhat empty. Your comments resonate with me now in a way they have never done before." Steve looked kindly at his fellow panelists. "Perhaps you are right. Perhaps my belief in the resurrection was a misguided and unnecessary distraction. If the bones are Jesus', which appears to be the case, then clearly I was wrong in my insistence. However, it is only fair for you to at least try to understand the perspective that has held me and the historical Christian faith together for centuries.

"For one thing, whatever is said about the resurrection, it cannot be downplayed in importance. As I read the New Testament, I hear a Jesus who claims to be God. In fact, the Jewish leaders' reaction to him and their accusations of blasphemy make sense only if this were his claim. Their response is understandable. I too might not have believed Jesus when he claimed to be God. But what you all are postulating, that Jesus was a good teacher or that he was a good man with great ideas, or something to that end, isn't an option. First of all, Jesus never gave us that option. His claim was that he was God, not merely a great teacher. Second of all, because of what Jesus did say about himself and because of what he got others to believe and do, we can hardly accept that he was a good man if *he knew he wasn't* who he claimed to be.

"Perhaps that's why I am more disturbed by the bones than any of you. I don't believe we can, with integrity, say Jesus was only a 'good man.' This person, Jesus, convinced too many people he was God. Every one of the disciples, except Judas, who killed himself, and John, who died in exile, were martyred defending the claim that Jesus was God. In fact, they claimed they saw him after his resurrection.

"Jesus' claim to be God has led millions to their deaths around the world, beginning with being fed to lions in first-century Rome until the present where, in many countries, people are still being imprisoned or executed for professing faith in Jesus. Jesus said he was God and he convinced people that he *was* God to the point they died for him. No, the option that he was a *good man* is not available. If he wasn't who he said he was – namely God – but convinced others that he was, Jesus could be nothing but an evil, self-consumed liar.

"Another option is that he was a lunatic – out of his mind. But if that were the case, why have so many other religions and people, including my fellow panelists, chosen to speak of him as a great teacher or a great man with great insights? No, he wasn't a madman. The only other option to me is that he was, in fact, who he claimed to be – God."

Lawrence wasn't pleased that one guest was dominating his airtime. But Steve's speech was so full of emotion it was holding everybody's attention.

"The resurrection was the proof that Jesus' claim to be God

was true. As the Christian church began to grow following Jesus' death, this new religion would have been easy to kill, once and for all. Any Roman official or temple guard or religious leader who wanted to restore order or silence this new Christian rabble that talked of a new lord and king would only have had to produce the body of Jesus to destroy what was called blasphemy by the Jewish leaders. If they could have gotten any one of the witnesses to his resurrection to recant, that might have done it. But no one recanted. They couldn't deny the truth . . . or so I thought."

Steve's disposition changed from one who was lecturing to one who was seeming to confess. "Now, with the discovery of these bones, I am left with either continuing to believe in a resurrection that has been disproved or to go to the first option and call Jesus a liar who led millions to a meaningless death. Can you understand why this is catastrophic to the members of my congregation? We have said we love Jesus. We are being forced to reject him as an evil liar. This is hard . . ."

Steve's voice trailed into silence. This silence was too much even for Lawrence to overcome. They sat staring at Steve, a man in need of sympathy and understanding, even from his adversaries.

Chapter 24

FRIENDS

"Jeez this is good! Do you eat like this all the time?" asked Wil between bites of pure pleasure. "And I'm not just saying this because I'm a little tired of TV dinners and fast food." Everyone gave a little chuckle.

Steve's family was also enjoying the lasagna, but Wil was in heaven.

Lasagna was Steve's specialty. He had worked on it for years. Wil had tasted it on previous visits to Steve's house, though not for about a year. Each time it seemed to get better. This was substantiated by the comments of Steve's wife and children. To Steve it was art. The layering process, the mixture of ricotta and mozzarella, and the anise-flavored sausage, all gave the lasagna a flavor that would make the finest Italian chef take note.

"Normally we eat better than this," said Steve as he feigned humility and subtly paid a compliment to Wendy. He also admitted this was the only thing he knew how to cook.

"It's amazing how he can make this taste so good and yet burn water every other time he tries to cook," added Wendy.

As Wil mopped up the last bit of sauce with his garlic bread, the kids asked to be excused and Wendy started clearing the table, knowing Wil and Steve had a lot to discuss.

"Why don't you go sit in the library? I'll try to keep the kids out of your hair."

Wil and Steve got up, thankful that Wendy was relieving them of dish duty. They were eager to talk. Reporters had interrupted their brief visit after the hearings. In the three days since then, Steve had been on the Royal Lawrence show and the crisis at his church had claimed the other fragmented hours.

The two took their coffee into the library.

"Thanks, Steve, for having me over."

"Anytime, Wil." They sat in wing chairs on either side of the coffee table. "How are you doing, anyway?"

Steve was usually the first one to ask the questions. This was partially due to his years in the pastorate and all the counseling he had done. More than that, though, Steve truly cared for Wil. He always had.

"I should ask you the same thing," responded Wil. "You got quite a grilling on the show. Man, this thing sure has taken on a life of its own."

"Are you surprised?"

Silence. Wil did not know what to say.

"Wil," Steve said as he leaned forward. "Tell me what you found."

Wil sat up straight and began to take on the aura of the world-renowned scholar with which he was most comfortable. He took a breath.

"A lot. It was amazing. After entering the tomb, we found two sets of bones. One of them belonged to Jesus. This was initially only substantiated by the tablet. Later we became absolutely certain. The other set, I'm convinced, are the remains of Joseph of Arimathea."

"I've heard a lot about the Jesus bones, but why do you think the other bones are Joseph's?"

Wil laid out his theory. "As you recall, the tomb Jesus' body was purported to have been buried in belonged to Joseph of

Arimathea, a wealthy Jewish sympathizer of 'the Jesus movement.' We found clothing fragments that obviously belonged to a rich man. On his finger was a ring marking him as a Jewish man of prominence. The tomb was in the precise area long suspected to be the field belonging to Joseph. I'm convinced Joseph went to pay his respects to his fallen prophet. Most likely, he would have gone to the tomb discreetly, without many people knowing, to avoid being ostracized.

"As he was leaving the burial chamber, something happened to cause the entrance to collapse, which killed him instantly and sealed the chamber off from the rest of the tomb. The Roman guards stationed at the tomb wouldn't have had the least bit of interest in digging up the body of a criminal or an obviously dead Jew. The burial chamber was conveniently and permanently secured. Shortly thereafter, the brick and mortar wall was put in place, probably so the other chamber could be used or maybe purely for aesthetics.

"My hunch is that the empty chamber was never used because it began to be regarded by some as the empty tomb of Jesus. Over time, as different conquering forces came and went through Jerusalem, memories faded even more and the resurrection myth grew. When the tomb was rediscovered in the nineteenth century, so much enthusiasm was present that no one bothered to thoroughly check the area. I'm convinced that, were it not for my chance discovery of the real tomb that night, the hidden chamber might never have been found."

"Do you really believe it's the body of Jesus?" Steve hoped he would hear a confession that Wil wasn't completely confident.

"I am absolutely convinced," said Wil. "Nothing else makes any sense."

"But why wouldn't the disciples have made an issue of the buried chamber?"

"What could they do?" responded Wil. "In fact, I find it interesting that the biblical account references a large stone being placed in front of the tomb. It also says the disciples found the tomb empty. Maybe the disciples never knew about the other chamber, the one we discovered, because it was closed off when its entrance collapsed. Perhaps the disciples sincerely thought the tomb was empty. Or maybe they simply couldn't get over their grief, and their wishful thinking caused them to create the story of the resurrection." Wil paused in his speculation. "But this isn't my issue. The fact is, I have found Jesus' bones. I don't know or care what happened with the disciples. At least we now know what happened to Jesus."

"Is there any chance there is more to the story, more clues in the chamber, that you didn't see in your first dig?"

Wil hesitated. This brought up a touchy subject for him. Ever since he had left the tomb the night they recovered the bones and went to the FBI lab, he had felt an urgency to go back. He didn't expect to find anything to cause him to change his mind. But the unfinished work bothered him. The virgin nature of the tomb, the dank smell, the hope of discovering other artifacts all burned within Wil. He had to get back to the dig.

But he couldn't. The team in the lab was still busy at work on the items they had already retrieved. There were meetings Wil was required to attend. And there were the congressional hearings. All these meant he couldn't leave. It was beyond frustrating to Wil. Even more troublesome was the way the bureaucracy seemed to be taking over his project. He was beginning to be concerned that he might not be allowed to go back into the tomb at all.

The bureaucracy had also become personal. Following the President's announcement and Wil's brief meeting with him, people in the lab changed. The President's minions were anything but friendly toward him. Wil was increasingly uneasy with certain members of his team. He was even worried that he might be removed from the project. But he didn't think he needed to burden Steve with his problems.

"I hope to get back to the dig sometime soon, but I'm so tied up in this congressional hearing thing and the research at the lab, it's difficult to see how I can."

Wil stopped. His goal had been to destroy the false religion of his father. He had done that. But what had he done to his friend? He glanced at Steve, whose deep tiredness was showing through. He hadn't seen Steve look like this since the death of his son, William. Before the find, Wil and Steve had disagreed, but each had been content and confident in his own worldview. After the find, Steve was forced into a situation that required a soul-searching Wil knew he himself had never gone through. He knew how strongly Steve had believed. He hadn't meant to hurt his friend.

"I'm sorry, Steve." This comment caught Steve by surprise. Wil went on. "I know what I've done affects you deeply. You're my closest friend. I didn't mean it to hurt you."

Steve looked back at Wil with the love of a father and a friend. "Wil, you didn't do anything to me. I've said all my life, 'I value truth.' If the truth is that Jesus isn't who he said he was and those are the bones of Jesus, then so be it. Eventually, after this phase passes, I'll probably even say thank you for helping me grow. Sure, I feel as if the wind has been knocked out of me. I feel numb. In a way, it's even a little scary. But truth is good, and truth is what I desire."

The two friends sat back in their chairs, both of their spirits in distress. They reached for their cups of coffee.

With a grin, Steve lowered his cup from his lips. "So . . . have you seen Hope?"

Always keep your head.

Chapter 25

THE LIMIT

Wil burst into Dennis Brock's office. Brock was the "White House liaison" who had come on the scene as a permanent member of the project five days before Wil's press announcement.

"What in the world is going on?" demanded Wil.

A man across the desk from Brock looked as if he'd been caught in an illicit affair.

Brock didn't miss a beat. "Dr. Wilson." It was as though Wil didn't look furious and this was an everyday greeting. "Allow me to introduce Dr. Mathias Mordecai. I've asked him to join our team. He comes to us from Yale and has agreed to help us out."

Wil was now the one who looked stunned. He wasn't sure if he should proceed with what he had come to do or greet his academic nemesis.

"Mathias? It's been a long time. Was it Stockholm?" And then Wil caught himself. This guy repulsed Wil but he was not going to let Mordecai or Brock sidetrack him. "Mathias, I don't want to sound rude, but would you please excuse us for a few minutes. I need to talk to Brock."

"Of course." Mordecai welcomed the invitation to go to safer ground. Like a man getting out of the way of his wife and mistress as the intensity increased, Dr. Mordecai slipped out of the office, leaving the two men standing.

Brock sat down behind the desk. "I was meaning to tell you.

We've decided to bring Dr. Mordecai here to assist you with some of your workload. We have all appreciated your hard work and long hours and we didn't think it was – "

"Cut the crap, Brock. I don't want him on my team. If you'd checked with me before you did another end run, you'd know that, but that isn't what I want to talk about."

Brock leaned back in his chair and put his hands in front of him, fingers steepled, with his index fingers touching his lips.

"What can I do for you, Wil?"

Wil hated this guy. He had slimed his way into the project. He had manipulated everything so that all information flowed through him, even while routinely reminding the team in public that Wil was the project's leader. More than once, Wil came close to chucking it all to haul off and deck him right between his smirking lips.

Getting back on track, Wil's teeth were clenched as he demanded, "What is this?" He slapped a three-page memo onto Brock's desk.

Brock was disturbed, though only a moment of slight hesitation revealed this. He tried to look surprised before he answered. "Nothing."

"Nothing! What do you mean, 'Nothing'?"

"I mean it's nothing."

Wil was not going to let that be the end. He was furious, and for a second it looked like Brock was fearful of what Wil might do.

"I mean it's nothing. We – "

"And stop using that pompous 'we'," Wil commanded, bracing himself with both hands on top of Brock's desk. Fury showing in his eyes, Wil leaned over the desk toward Brock.

Brock had regained his control. He calmly stated, "I merely thought it would be a good idea to start documenting our phone calls."

"Our phone calls! The only phone number I see being documented is mine!"

"Dr. Wilson, I assure you this is standard protocol for a project of this magnitude. With the congressional hearings and all the accountability related to this project, we need to keep track of costs."

"Come off it! You idiot bureaucrats are getting out of control. I know how much money you guys are spending on this project. Maybe the congressman is right. Certainly 12.8 million dollars is a ton of money if all it can buy is a stuffed suit like you and a third-rate archaeologist like Mordecai. And now you're playing stupid games." Wil paused to catch his breath.

"Tracking my phone calls! I've about had it! I know I ticked your boss off when I made the announcement. I know you political mongrels want to spin and control this thing as much as you can. But at least have the courtesy of being straight with me. Are you going to remove me from this project? Is that what you want?"

Wil's real concern was purely this. Was he going to be pushed off the project and not allowed to be a part of the research? The thought of it terrified him. Seeing his long-time antagonist, Mordecai, jawing with Mr. Slimebucket pretty much told him his hunches were likely to be true. Wil was so angry he knew he was not being as articulate as he felt he had to be.

"Absolutely not. We know you are the director of this project and you have done outstanding work." Brock was back to his smooth and slithering self. "That's part of the reason we brought in Dr. Mordecai. We want to free you from some of the day-to-day tasks and let you concentrate more on the research related to your discovery."

Wil knew the conversation was lost. This guy could change the direction of a charging bull on a narrow street in Pamplona. He was good. It felt useless to continue.

"Knock it off, Brock." Wil's veins were standing out on his neck, though his volume had decreased slightly. "I'm fed up with you and your bureaucratic stonewalling and your asinine word games. Furthermore, your pathetic groveling and crawling for your boss is sickening. I've about reached my limit. Any more of this crap," he pointed at the memo, "and I'll take more drastic measures."

Wil turned and walked out of the office.

As Brock was reaching for the phone, Wil barged back into the room. "And I do *not* want Mordecai on this project. Got it?" He slammed the door as he left.

Wil went to his office and did what he always did in a situation like this. He reached for the phone to call Beth. He would have to call her at home, as it would be nearly nine p.m. in Israel. But then he set the phone down, thinking it might not be such a good idea. He decided to call her from a pay phone. They would have a harder time monitoring him, at least so he thought. He got up and told his assistant he was going to lunch. Wil had barely left the room when his assistant dialed Brock.

On the drive to the restaurant, where Wil had no intention of eating but which had a secluded phone booth, he noticed the phone number on the yellow "sticky" note stuck to his dashboard. Steve had looked up the number and handed it to Wil as he left the Haltermans' house a few days ago. Wil didn't have the resolve to toss the number or the courage to call it.

As he was debating what to do, he noticed a car that seemed to be following him. When the car turned right and disappeared he shook it off, thinking his paranoia was getting out of control. He was an archaeologist for heaven's sake! Mustering his courage, he dialed the number on his cell phone. He didn't notice the other car, which had begun to follow him after the first car disappeared.

146

"Hello."
"Hello . . . Hope?
"Yes?"
"This is Wil."
Silence
"Wil?"

Meanwhile, Brock was on his phone. "Kathreen, this is Brock. I think we have a problem."

Perspective changes.

Chapter 26

AT STARBUCKS

"So? You said you wanted to talk." Hope was in control of the 'let's-get-together-and-talk' meeting Wil had initiated the previous afternoon from his car phone. She was still surprised.

Starbucks was crowded. Wil could never get over the prices these guys could get for a cup of coffee. He told others, and himself, the coffee in Jerusalem tasted better, was more rewarding to drink, and was less expensive than the liquid gold squeezed out by the millions of espresso machines in the United States. Nevertheless, the aroma of freshly brewed Colombian was delicious.

Wil felt intimidated by all the people crowded around their little round tables, sitting on the wooden stools with wrought-iron backs that passed as chairs. He preferred to avoid crowds. However, this setting offered plenty of acceptable distractions, since he felt even more nervous in the presence of the one person sharing his table. He struggled to say something, anything, to his past love. It was a far cry from the numerous times he and Hope had sat in cafes throughout Europe. Then they would easily communicate volumes, as they looked at each other, content and comfortable in each other's presence.

"I figured . . . that since I was in town . . . I should . . . at least get in touch with you . . . since I never wrote back to you . . . after your letter." Wil knew he was babbling, and kept his hands under the table to hide the sweat on his palms. *Great!* he thought. *I sound like an idiot.*

Hope regretted sending that letter now. Why had she told him she still had feelings for him? Why hadn't she been stronger? She could feel the color rise in her cheeks. Keeping her voice even, she said, "That was considerate of you. It's been a long time." Pause.

"Um . . . y'know Wil, you really look great."

Wil was embarrassed, though encouraged. He welcomed her kind words and loved her voice. He lifted his eyes to meet hers. Seeing the flush on her cheeks, a flood of memories threatened to overwhelm him. "I love you" was all he could think of saying, so he said nothing.

"Do you still have Napoleon?" Hope broke the silence. This would be a neutral enough subject to let Wil, and also her, feel more comfortable.

"I sure do," said Wil. The tension lessened. "That old hairball has turned out to be quite the cat. He not only keeps the mice down, but he's pretty nice to have around. When I come home from work, the darn cat treats me like a king. He fetches my slippers – "

"No!" Hope retorted in disbelief.

"And climbs in my lap and helps me unwind." Wil finished his sentence proudly.

"Napoleon actually *fetches* your slippers for you?" Hope was flabbergasted. "Are you talking about the same cat that ate nearly every pair of shoes I owned?"

"Yep." Wil said with a laugh.

"I can't believe it!" She looked shocked. "He's lucky I didn't skin him after he destroyed my favorite Birkenstocks."

"It took three years in Jerusalem, a dozen pairs of shoes, a trip to the vet to get him fixed, and threats to feed him to the wild dogs, but he eventually turned into a great cat." Wil sounded like a boasting father.

There was a moment of awkward silence as they looked into each other's eyes. Hope glanced down. Wil reached for his latte.

"How's your new job?" asked Wil. He took a sip, having steered the conversation in another direction.

"I was waiting for you to ask me that," said Hope. Though still mildly light-headed, she took on the posture of a defense attorney having to deal with an unfavorable piece of evidence. She had been waiting to face the inevitable. Wil knew how apolitical Hope had been at Oxford.

"It's kind of hard to believe I'm right in the middle of D.C. working for a politician, isn't it?" She paused and looked at the jury for sympathy.

Wil only smiled.

"Are you surprised?" she asked with a lopsided grin. She was hoping Wil had forgotten the "I will *never* go into politics" speech she had made on too many occasions.

He hadn't.

Hope wanted to get this out of the way. It had been a youthful promise anyway. She rationalized, "But this is different." She had convinced herself that what she was doing with Congressman Newcastle was attacking all that was wrong with the American political system, epitomized in the disreputable Senator Brown.

Wil was still smiling.

Hope continued. "I was as surprised as anybody when Congressman Newcastle asked me to help him unseat Senator Brown and he told me his reasons. It sounded so much like the ideals we shared back at Oxford."

Wil decided to end the suffering. "Hope, it's okay." He was still grinning though. "You don't need to apologize."

Hope bristled.

Wil added, "I hope Congressman Newcastle wins."

"I wasn't apologizing," she replied stiffly, but thankful the subject was behind them.

"Yes, you were," chided Wil with a different look and the tone that used to move the two younger lovebirds beyond any conflicts that arose. "But, more importantly, do you like your job?"

"Yes." Hope matched his look. "For once in my life, I actually think what I'm doing is important."

Wil lifted his shoulders a little and looked at Hope. "But wasn't your column on the pollution in Boston Harbor important? Or the series you wrote on welfare reform?"

Hope looked at Wil slyly. It was her turn.

"How did you know about my series on the harbor?" In her letter she had mentioned only the series on welfare reform.

"We do get U.S. newspapers in Israel, you know," was his lame attempt to cover up his gaff. Wil was regretting he had disclosed this tidbit of information to Hope's astute reporter's instincts. He didn't want to tell her he had been following her career and had read nearly everything she had ever written. It was kind of a secret hobby even Beth didn't know about. He was now on the receiving end of the smile.

Hope sensed there was much more to the story than Wil was letting on. Looking at him over the rim of her cup, Hope now was not so disappointed that she had shared her feelings in her letter.

"So you like this Newcastle guy?" asked Wil forcing the conversation back in a direction in which he felt more comfortable.

"I do," responded Hope, letting Wil off the hook. "He's a man of integrity. He has a lot of strong opinions which, fortunately, I agree with – for the most part. But beyond all that, he's a good man. He wants to do what's right."

"Do you think he'll win the election?"

"As I see it now, we don't stand much of a chance, particularly since the President is backing Brown so strongly." Hope raised her voice, but not enough for others to hear as she narrowed her eyes at Wil. "And if you hadn't given the President and Senator Brown their 'Lead America into the Post-Christian Age platform,' we might have had a chance of winning."

Wil knew Hope was teasing him, but he still couldn't get over how bewildering it was that his find had turned into such a political bonanza.

"I know." Wil sighed. "I can hardly believe it myself. Who would've thought that finding the bones of Jesus would impact the United States' presidential and senatorial elections? What's amazing to me is how much hay the President has made with it." He stopped, and then went on almost to himself.

"And I can't believe how discovering the most important archaeological find in modern times has ended up getting me into such a precarious position."

"What do you mean?"

"Oh nothing," said Wil with a wave of a hand. He had already said too much.

"Yeah, right! I can still see right through you William Wilson. What do you mean, 'precarious position'?"

Wil looked into Hope's eyes and, hesitant, leaned forward as if this would make his words more believable. He hadn't seen Hope for almost ten years, yet somehow he knew he could still trust her.

"Hope, it . . . it's odd. Do you remember how the President said he was behind my announcement?"

"Yes. It only replayed on the news about a thousand times."

"The fact of the matter is the President was going to try to cover up my find. He thought it was too much of a political hot potato to let out before the election. It was only when I was convinced that the bureaucrats and their government machines were going to silence my discovery that I went public."

"Why would he want to cover it up?"

"Heck, I don't know. Maybe he didn't want to upset the political apple cart before the election. All I know is, he *definitely* did not want to go public with the discovery. It was bizarre."

"But the President said he supported your announcement and that he was fully behind your actions."

"Not true." Wil shook his head. "In fact, I really ticked him off. When I met with the President following my announcement, everyone came away thinking we were all one big happy family. Wrong. The President said something to me that has bothered me ever since."

"What'd he say?"

"It was probably nothing, except . . ." Wil hesitated, thinking he'd sound like some paranoid weirdo. "Except after that meeting, I've felt as if I'm being excluded from things – meetings, communiqués, memos. I often find out about these only by chance. They seem to be diverted from me. Some of the people in the lab are acting differently toward me. They're tracking my phone calls. Sometimes, I feel like I'm being followed."

"What did *he* say?" Hope would not let this one go.

"I was sitting with him and some of his advisors after the public relations picture session. He talked about leading the world into a new age and about teamwork." Wil leaned forward and lowered his voice as if it were a secret. "Then, he looked straight at me and told me I should have checked with him before I 'changed the world'."

"What's that supposed to mean?" Hope lifted her eyebrows.

"He said he doesn't 'appreciate surprises'."

"Uh huh."

"To tell you the truth, I'm certain it was a threat. At first I thought he was joking. I've concluded that I'm not on the most powerful man in the world's list of favored people."

Hope and Wil were distracted by the commotion at the front door. Congressman Jones had walked in and the shop owner was telling the press entourage to stay out and wait on the sidewalk. Based on appearances, this was a normal routine. The congressman went to the counter as if he had done so a number of times before.

"Will you look at that?" said Wil. The congressman was standing at the counter looking like anything but a right-wing fanatic. "I wonder if he'll lay into me here like he has up there on the Hill." Wil's blood pressure rose.

Hope was quiet. If Congressman Newcastle's campaign needed anything, it needed to avoid his chief of staff standing up in the middle of Starbucks and getting into a major confrontation with Congressman Jones, her boss's long-time adversary from South Carolina.

After paying for his coffee and turning to look for a place to sit, the congressman's eyes squarely met Hope's and Wil's. The place was packed. Call it a coincidence or a curse, the only empty seat was one small corner table right next to the one at which Hope and Wil were sitting.

The routine clatter of the coffee shop faded into the background as they each considered their next move. Who was going to blink?

Congressman Jones felt trapped. He could go back to the reporters and not enjoy his coffee. Or he could sit next to the chief of staff of his long-term adversary, who was with the man he had recently browbeaten in the congressional hearings. He sighed, walked to the table, and sat down.

"Hello, Miss Fairview, Dr. Wilson," said the congressman, nodding courteously.

Hope was surprised he called her by name. She had never talked with him, though she had sent him many letters on behalf of Congressman Newcastle. It was a peculiar thing in Washington. Even adversaries had to work together at times, particularly when they were on so many of the same committees.

"I'm sorry I had to come off so strong at the hearings, Dr. Wilson. Please understand that it is nothing personal."

Hmm? thought Wil. Is that the way D.C. works? First you pummel someone in public and then apologize in private. Or, as in the case of the President's words to Wil, vice versa.

Meeting the congressman's eyes, Wil remained silent.

"How goes the campaign?" The congressman addressed his question to Hope.

Hope was caught off-guard. First of all, what was she doing being drawn into a conversation with someone she usually saw as the enemy? And why was he being so nice?

"Fine," said Hope guardedly.

"Can I tell you something, off the record?" asked the congressman.

Hope wasn't sure what to make of this, but she nodded with polite interest.

"I sure hope Congressman Newcastle upsets Senator Brown."

Hope gasped. She could hardly believe her ears and, before she had time to catch her breath, the congressman continued.

"Your boss and I disagree on nearly every issue that has ever come before us. However, I believe he's a man of integrity, and in this place that matters even to those who are on the opposite end of the stick."

The congressman was now on a voluntary data dump. Neither Hope nor Wil knew what to do.

"And, Dr. Wilson, I know it might not be easy to understand, but I truly do not harbor any negative feelings against you. My concern is that the behavior of our government must be consistent with the laws passed by the Congress or put forth in our Constitution. My issue is that government funds were spent on something I believe is of largely religious significance. If the funds had been used to dig up an idol of Buddha or to translate the Koran, I would have had the same objection. This particular issue is undeniably more personal to me than those would be, but the real issue has to do with the separation of church and state. Your discovery is what brought the issue to light." He lifted his coffee and took a swallow.

This information didn't make Wil any less frustrated with what was going on, nor did he agree with the underlying conspiracy the congressman thought was there. But, he did see a side of the congressman he had not expected. This man was sincere. He really thought he was doing the right thing.

Wil was preparing to say something, though he wasn't sure what, but the reporters outside had become restless. Congressman Jones, the object of their attention, knew it was time for him to leave. He graciously thanked Wil and Hope for letting him join them, stood and walked outside, stopping only to stuff his large paper latte cup into the trash bin near the front door. His "No comment," trailed to silence as the door shut behind him.

Wil had already moved his chair so his back was to the door and was relieved that the congressman remained their target. If the reporters found out that Wil had been with the congressman and the chief of staff for the congressman's adversary, no shopkeeper would have been able to keep them outside.

Ignorance is bliss

until you realize you are ignorant.

Chapter 27

SLEUTH

What the press didn't notice, the State Department snoops did.

But they were not sure what to do with their new information. From the time Wil had called Hope on his car phone until their meeting at Starbucks the following morning, the two hacks were uncertain how to categorize Hope. It seemed to be a purely personal contact, and they were so focused on not losing track of Wil that they didn't pay much attention to who Wil was meeting. To them, she was simply a pretty woman. They passed the contact off as, "The ol' guy is finally feeling his hormones."

The appearance of Congressman Jones was of greater interest to them, but the interaction looked like happenstance. They weren't suspicious about this either. In their documentation, they merely noted: "Target at Starbucks with lady friend. Apparent chance encounter with Congressman Jones."

Wil and Hope exited Starbucks and walked back toward his hotel, which was across from the Indonesian Embassy near Dupont Circle on Embassy Row. On the way, Wil escorted Hope to the Dupont Circle Metro Station. As she headed toward the ticket gate, one of the men tailing Wil mused, "I wonder if we'll see that babe again?" They still didn't think of the situation as anything more than a hormonal treat. On the other hand, they did pay a little too much attention to how nice her backside looked as she descended the escalator. Wil, who also was keenly interested in her appearance, happened to notice the two suits watching her. When they turned back toward Wil, he was looking straight at them. Their eyes met. The two not-so-seasoned stalkers tried to look inconspicuous, pretending they had not been noticed. One fumbled for change in his pockets. The other looked back at the escalators.

Wil kept his cool and casually began to walk to his hotel, deliberately not looking back. When the Hilton bellman held the door for him, Wil glanced over his shoulder. The two men were standing across the street looking at the address on the embassy's front gate.

Wil failed to extend his usual greetings to the lobby staff as he headed to the elevator and pushed "3." His hand was shaking. In the mirrored elevator wall he noticed the beads of sweat on his forehead. When the elevator door opened at the third floor, he looked up and down the hallway before stepping out. He went directly to his room, his magnetic key card ready. He walked in, turned the TV to CNN and, for the first time, released his anxiety as he collapsed on the end of his bed.

After a moment of catching his breath and his thoughts, he slowly stood up and began a casual search of his room. He found one bug and left it in place. His fears were confirmed. He concluded it would be best not to change his routine, and he got ready to go to the lab.

That day, Wil noticed greater hesitancy in some of his staff. Brock's greeting was in his normal, hypocritically chipper tone. They exchanged a few words. Nothing out of the ordinary, though Wil thought Brock's grin was unusually smug. After a few moments they parted, as usual. Brock entered his office and closed the door. Through the glass-paneled wall Wil saw him pick up the phone.

Wil headed to the lab, again as usual, to check on the status of one of the carbon-dating reports he had been waiting for. Halfway down the corridor, a phone's ring caught his ear. It came from an office that belonged to one of the people whose names or tasks he didn't know. Wil surmised this guy was extremely tight with Brock, based on the number of times they were in each other's offices. He stopped and cautiously stepped toward the door, which was slightly ajar. Wil looked through the crack and listened.

"Brock? . . . Yes, I'm alone. . . . When? What kind of accident? . . . I understand." He hung up, took his coat from the back of his chair, pulled something from his desk drawer, and headed toward the door.

Wil was barely able to hide behind the door as it swung open into the hallway. The man was putting his other arm into its coat sleeve as he briskly left his office. He swung the door closed, leaving Wil exposed, standing with his back pressed against the wall, his breath frozen. Fortunately, the man was heading down the hall in the other direction, and in his intense concentration he failed to notice Wil or that his door had not latched.

Daring to breathe again as the stranger turned the corner, Wil reached for the door and slipped into the office. He wasn't sure what he was doing, but he felt compelled. He opened the drawer from which he had seen the man take something. He found a partially empty box of gun clips. No gun.

The next drawer had some files. He pulled the phone logs. As he had suspected, only his calls were being tracked. There was a file containing pictures of him, beginning a few days before his announcement and becoming more exhaustive as time passed. There was even a picture of Hope and him leaving Starbucks that morning. A number of memos with the seal of the Office of the President also caught his attention.

Then he found a copy of the staffing memo he had intercepted a few days ago. He decided to examine it a little more closely. The handwritten notes on the memo piqued his curiosity. At the top it said, "Bones Project Staffing." He was particularly puzzled with the figure of "100G" next to about two-thirds of the names. Wil knew some of the names, but there were many more names on the staffing list than employees in the lab working on his project. He counted the names with "100G" next to them. Ninety-two.

The next document he pulled terrified him. It was a memo to Kathreen Steele and dated the previous day. It read:

> Kathreen:
>
> As of this date, we have been able to support the campaign with $9.2 million via payroll diversions.
>
> This should be good news to the President.
>
> Chet
>
> cc: Brock

It was obvious. Ninety-two names times 100 grand equaled $9.2 million. They were funding the President's re-election campaign from Wil's project. Wil's mind was flying. He remembered Brock's peculiar look of concerned shock the previous day, when he made reference to the congressman and the large amounts of money they were spending on the project. Did they think he knew?

He sank into the chair. The congressman had been hounding everyone about the fact that the money *had* been spent, not *how* it had been spent. If Jones only knew.

Wil's paranoia turned to terror. It only got worse as he heard steps approaching the office. He dived under the desk and was relieved when the passerby moved on past the office toward the lab.

He could still hear the footsteps when his watch began to beep. He caught it before its third beep, but he knew the person in the hallway must have heard the sound coming from the darkened office. Wil was completely still, heart pounding and palms wet. He listened. The steps slowed and then returned to normal before continuing down the hall. He exhaled and crawled out from under the desk. He waited for his heart to return to normal before standing. He had to steady himself against the desk, his legs unable to bear his weight.

After regaining his strength and his wits, Wil left the office, making sure the door was securely latched, and proceeded to the lab as if nothing had happened.

Throughout the rest of the day, while every nerve and muscle in his body was telling him to flee, Wil kept his composure and pretended he was none the wiser. No one knew that, while discussing reports, attending meetings, and talking to the other scientists, he was formulating a plan he knew had to be implemented that night. His visit to the multimedia room, where they were analyzing the shroud, netted him a tape recorder. His long walks down the halls of the complex allowed him ample planning time. His trips to the bathroom provided him with some time for recording. By the end of the day he was ready, but he was also scared to death.

That evening as the door of the hotel elevator closed he overheard the bellman say to the desk clerk, "It's nice to see the Doc back to his normal self. We were a little concerned about him last night."

Things seemed to be going well. Wil was ready.

After waiting in his room for ten minutes, he picked up the phone and dialed.

"Hope?"

"Is that you, Wil?"

"Uh, H-Hope." Wil stuttered. He was pretty impressed with how real his act was sounding. "I have to see you. My heart's been pounding ever since I saw you this morning. I can't stop thinking about you. I love you, Hope, and I can't hide it anymore."

It was hard to tell whether Hope or the two men listening to the call were more stunned with Wil's pathetically poor Casanova act and blunt lovemaking.

One of the eavesdroppers, Officer Jerome Jefferson, looked to his superior, Sergeant Stu Randolf, and cracked, "I guess you were right. This guy's hormones finally got cranked up. Can't say I really blame him. She's a beauty!"

"Shut up! I'm listening," snapped the sergeant.

Hope still had not spoken. For one thing, she was having a hard time believing it was Wil since he had never talked like this before. Plus, it had been ten years.

"Hope, I know you have the same feelings for me. I want you tonight. I want you now."

Hope was blushing and perturbed. Had she not detected something was wrong, she probably would have hung up.

"I'm in room 305. Please get here as quick as you can." Wil put down the receiver.

"Presumptuous pervert, isn't he?" snorted Randolf. "I guess we'll see if this chick is as strange as the good doc."

Wil walked over to the radio next to the bed and turned on a classical station. It was unusually loud, which Wil hoped wouldn't be too suspicious. He needed the volume to be high to cover up the sounds he would be making in the next few minutes. Sergeant Randolf assumed Wil was trying to set a mood.

Wil put a small note in the door jam, and placed a larger note on the table, in clear view of the door. He set the tape recorder on the edge of the table next to the note. Then he began his escape.

Meanwhile, Randolf and Jefferson were laying odds on whether or not "the chick" would show.

Wil dimmed the lights and carefully put his prepared day-pack on his back. He barely parted the curtains, opened the window, and crawled out onto the ledge. He had been on a number of digs that required pretty clever footwork to get around dangerous drops, but even they were not as threatening as the thirty-foot drop to the narrow, and fortunately dark, alley below his room.

Wil edged his way past one room. A businessman, still in his three-piece suit, his tie loosened and his collar unbuttoned, was fixated on a rerun of *Star Trek*. Next Wil passed a vacant room, after which he was able to fumble down the drainpipe to the alley. He made his way to Dupont Circle Metro Station, caught the Red Line to Farragut North Station, where he switched to the Blue Line that took him to Washington National Airport even before Hope was able to get to his hotel room. With Hope's arrival, the activity in the parked van became animated.

"Pay up, buddy. There she is! And man, oh man, does she look fine!"

Randolf responded to the triumphant subordinate with a backhanded slap across Jefferson's chest. The sergeant began to dig for his wallet. "Well, at least this evening won't be as boring as the last five," he grumbled, beginning to reveal a peeping-tom personality and a lack of professional standards and thoroughness.

"And she made it in just under sixty minutes." Jefferson looked at his boss. "Unless I'm mistaken, that's another twenty bucks."

With a grunt, Randolf reopened his wallet, wanting to get past this part and hear what would happen next.

"Wil?" Hope said as she pushed open the door that had been left barely ajar for her. She picked up the piece of paper, which had fallen to the ground as the door opened.

SAY NOTHING ELSE. READ THE NOTE ON THE TABLE.

Hope's investigative reporter spirit had surfaced after its respite in politics. She was prepared for anything, or so she thought. Hope picked up the note from the table and read the first few lines silently. Then she read what followed, out loud, in as convincing a tone as she could.

"What do you mean, no words?" said Hope, having a hard time adjusting to her character. "Wil . . . this is awfully kinky. Okay . . . okay . . . but Wil I . . ." She stopped speaking under cover of the radio music.

The calm reporter-turned-actress read her script to herself:

THE ROOM IS BUGGED

BE CAREFUL

1) My life is in danger and I'm sorry I had to do it this way.

2) Turn the tape on in 3 minutes and follow along with the script.

3) I need at least 12 hours.

4) I will call you at your place at 8 p.m. Thursday.

5) I meant the part about not being able to stop thinking about you.

Hope sat in the chair next to the table and sighed. In all the hours she had thought and dreamed about seeing Wil again, she never, in her wildest imagination, thought it would play out like this.

She had one minute until she had to turn the tape on. *What's going on?* She remembered Paris and Oxford. She forgot Heathrow. She remembered Starbucks, and smiled. Glancing through the script, she readied herself for the performance of her life. She had significant objections with the playwright, but she was already on stage and it was too late for that. *What the heck, I might as well play it to the hilt for the audience, whoever they are,* she thought as she reached to turn on the tape player. *At least it's interesting.*

"I love you, Hope." Wil spoke from the tape recorder.

Hope read her next line. "But Wil, it's been so long. . . . We've hardly spoken."

The tape responded, "Then let's keep it that way . . . at least for tonight."

Hope was aghast at Wil's dialogue. Was this the twilight zone or had she been mysteriously sucked into some cheap romance novel? Even in their most passionate times, Wil had never talked like this

"Kiss me, Wil," read Hope, trying to sound seductive.

"No words then?"

"Agreed." Then, in as sweet and consenting a voice as Hope could muster, she said, "I've missed you, Wil," and turned off the tape as the directions told her.

Hope then did her best to make the sounds of clothes coming off, passionate lovemaking, and an occasional giggle or moan after which she would pause and start up again so the listeners would not get suspicious. Hope promised herself that, somehow, if this was ever sorted out, she was going to make Wil pay in spades for what he had asked her to do for him.

Eventually, somewhat disgusted, Hope fell asleep.

Meanwhile, the listeners were proud of their target and wished him a good night's rest.

Hope turned the tape player on again at seven-thirty a.m. Wil's voice announced he was going to take a shower. Hope turned on the shower, then the morning news, with the TV's volume louder than it needed to be. She announced, per the script, that she was leaving and could hardly wait to see him later that day for lunch.

"Call me," she yelled to the empty shower as she gathered up the tape player, notes, and script before leaving the hotel room. She made her way back to her apartment, where she began what she determined was going to look like a completely normal day.

At eight o'clock, Wil was still in the shower. By eight-thirty, the day sergeant, who had relieved Randolf and Jefferson at eight from the night crew, was suspicious. By nine, the eavesdroppers received permission to enter the room. They found the shower still running and CNN still on the TV. The sergeant picked up the phone and called his boss.

Hope's interview with the FBI agents that afternoon went exceptionally well. She had been on the other end of so many interviews that she was able to convince them not only that she had no idea what they were talking about, but also that she was more than a little miffed Wil had stood her up.

"He said we'd have lunch together!" She gestured to how nicely she had dressed for the occasion.

The interviewers could see this was one angry female who resented being stood up by a sicko like Wil. They didn't bother to put a tail on her.

Chapter 28

BETH

Beth could hardly believe she was standing in front of a security team in a skin-tight, low-cut red dress and high heels, with a cigarette hanging from her mouth. She kind of liked the hair, the way it curled forward in wisps and emphasized her eyes and cheekbones. Assuming she came out of this foolishness alive, she planned to keep the hairstyle.

She hadn't heard much from Wil over the past month. This was unusual. She assumed it was all the excitement and enthusiasm about his recent find. The fact was, his absence allowed her to catch up on some of her own work. It also made her job a little easier. She could legitimately say she couldn't reach Wil when someone wanted to schedule a meeting or speaking arrangement. It had been three days since they last talked – a rather scattered call from a phone booth. Beth had received that call as she was getting ready for bed. Wil said something about things not going as planned. She concluded that the situation was getting a little tense. Then, earlier this evening, Wil had called again.

"Hi, Beth."

"Where are you, Dr. Wilson?"

"I'm in the lab at the Institute."

"I thought you were in Washington." She was actually glad to hear he was back.

"Beth," Wil continued, not addressing her underlying question of what he was doing back in Israel. "I need you to do something for me."

"Is it illegal or immoral?" Beth responded with a smile Wil couldn't see but somehow felt from the other end of the line. She was still having a hard time grasping that her boss was back in Israel. She was even more unprepared for the next question.

"Do you still have that red dress?"

"What?" Beth was puzzled. She didn't know her boss had noticed the red dress she had worn only once. It had been her first and only order from *Victoria's Secret*, and it pushed her style envelope a little further than she felt comfortable. She decided that, though she looked "killer" in the dress, it really wasn't her and she put it in the back of her closet.

"I need you to put that red dress on and get all fixed up and look your sexiest . . ."

Beth had no clue where Wil was going with this. There never had been, nor did Beth ever think there would be, any romance between them. But perhaps the pressure of the last two months was too much for the good doctor.

". . . and meet me at the Garden Tomb in two hours."

Beth's mouth opened wide without any breath or sound coming out. She switched the phone to the other ear as if this would somehow make things clearer.

"And," Wil continued as if Beth wasn't going to ask why or what in Hades he was talking about, "do you think you could bring some cigarettes?"

Beth had given them up five years ago and Wil knew that.

"You'll need them tonight. This is really important." Wil's tone was more serious than Beth had ever heard.

"Hold it, William Wilson." Beth had never called him William before. But she figured his unannounced return to

Israel and asking her, over the phone, to show up in a sexy red dress smoking cigarettes at a two thousand-year-old tomb under heavy security was a little out of the ordinary. "What is going on?" she demanded.

"Beth, I'm in trouble. I think I may even be in danger. The American government is going to remove me from the project. They haven't gotten over my announcement to the press. But, there's more to it. I know this all must sound crazy, but I really need you to do this."

That was all it took. Beth told Wil she would be there, hung up the phone and went to her closet.

Discovery is a beginning, not an end.

Chapter 29

THE COMMANDO

So, there she was. Wil had already told Beth, more than once, that she really looked great. Beth thought so too. Wil had briefly described the situation. Her job was to distract the small contingent of soldiers acting as security guards, while Wil made his way into the tomb.

He had already made it to the point where his next move was to crawl to within thirty feet of the far corner of the chain-link fence the Israeli secret police had put up after taking control of the site. At the signal, he was to run toward the fence, scramble under it, crawl through the perimeter area to the Garden Wall, and climb over the wall, all without being noticed. No problem. In the way the mind has of providing comic relief at tense moments, it occurred to Wil that he could describe this as his first experience in "commando archaeology." At that moment, though, he was terrified. Would they shoot him if they caught him?

Beth was doing great. She hadn't lost her ability to do things with cigarette smoke that would make any arsonist or artist envious. The guards were impressed and they appreciated the midnight distraction on this otherwise boring assignment. Between the giggling and teasing, they made failed attempts to outdo her with one of their own smoking tricks. The laughter drew the other guards, intrigued by the sounds of a giddy woman. She beat back any challenges the guards attempted. Their male egos were determined not to let themselves be out-done by a woman. Maybe it was merely the enjoyment of the innocent flirtation with this sexy woman in the red dress. Whatever it was, it was working and Beth was feeling proud of her performance.

Wil readied himself. Beth gave the signal. One of the hard-est parts of turning and running toward the tomb was not watch-ing Beth. Where in the world had she learned to do that? The seven guards surrounded her, trying to blow their own smoke rings. Beth had them all watch her as she took a new cigarette, exhaled, placed it between her lips, and then began to inhale. Wil knew that in about thirty seconds the entire cigarette would be gone, including the butt. He had that long to be under the fence and over the wall. Beth's distraction had to work, since this was their only plan to keep the guards occupied while he made his break. She had done this trick for him once before on a bet. After she threw up and Wil nearly died laughing, she decided to give up smoking. They were both hoping she would not throw up tonight.

Wil lost a few seconds trying to time the searchlight pattern. He made it under the fence and struggled to get over the wall. Beth still held the guards' attention. Wil more or less fell down the other side precisely as the light hit the top of the wall. He began to crawl as fast as he could with his black daypack filled with supplies on his back. The black ski mask felt terrible on his face, but he had seen it done this way in movies and figured it would help. The sunglasses made it harder to see, but they cov-ered the rest of his white face and eyes. He felt pretty proud of his camouflage attire. *Not bad for an amateur,* he thought.

Whenever the searchlight swept by, Wil lay perfectly still. The rock fence and the bushes provided decent cover. Wil knew he had to make good time. He also knew he had to time it perfectly. He had to cross the fifteen meters of open area, scale the second fence that had been installed immediately in front of the tomb, and get into the tomb without anyone seeing him when the searchlight illuminated the tomb's entrance.

Beth was going to occupy the guards for exactly forty-five minutes from the time she caused her first diversion. This matched the interval between the regular patrols of the garden area by one of the guards. She would then have to make a scene in order for Wil to get out of the tomb, over the first fence, over the wall, and under the second fence, while dodging the searchlight pattern and without the guards' seeing him.

Wil made it over the second fence and into the tomb. Immediately after the next pass of the light, he was able to hang a black curtain over the tomb's entrance and over the small window carved out to the right of the opening. This would shut in the light of his electric lantern and the flashes from his camera.

Wil shrugged the daypack off and took out his camera. He took picture after picture. After exhausting his roll of film, he sat on the ground in the opening of the new chamber with his back to the antechamber and the original tomb. Facing the newly discovered chamber, he tried to imagine the situation two thousand years ago. He calculated he had about twenty-five minutes.

His lantern-style flashlight rested on the stone bench in the middle of the room. What was this table for? It must have been the place they would lay a body while they applied the burial spices and wrapped the body in its shroud.

Wil was trying to visualize the night the ceiling had collapsed and killed Joseph, trapping his body with the corpse of Jesus. He looked across the table to the burial ledge on the other side of the chamber, where they had found the Jesus bones. This was a unique perspective – the lighting, dust motes slowly circling, and no one else in the room. It was beautiful. He tried to imagine what it was like the day they put Jesus' body there and what might have caused the cave entrance to crumble.

It was quiet. He could barely hear the distant sounds of the guards talking with Beth.

Wil imagined Joseph paying his respects to Jesus and walking around the table toward the door. Gazing at the pile of rocks, pebbles and dust from which they had dug Joseph's body, Wil's eye caught something unusual. The untouched part of the pile had a slight bulge. So much attention and care had been taken in extracting Joseph's body that they had moved only about one-third of the mound. The rest was still piled as it had been for two thousand years. He thought about physics and erosion and the normal slope of fallen rocks. *What is it?*

Wil checked his watch. Twenty minutes left.

"What the heck? There's one way to find out," Wil muttered out loud as he stepped toward the mound. With a grunt, he began to move rocks. He was tossing and throwing and digging as fast as he could. Within minutes, the sweat was dripping from his face, his muscles ached, and he had given up trying to keep the dust out of his eyes. He had to find out if anything was under there.

Scooping away a handful of pebbles and dust, his hand felt a flat surface. He moved more rocks, his excitement rising.

It was a large stone box, about the size of a two-drawer file cabinet on its side. No doubt. It was a "bones box." He recalled how these were used by first-century Jewish families who owned a grave or a tomb. They would put the bones of the previously deceased family members into the bones box prior to the next body being placed in the tomb. It kept them safe, but it also allowed for a tomb to be used over and over by the family.

He began to remove the stone slab that served as the lid, not an easy task due to its weight and because the precise fit made it difficult to grip. He was a treasure hunter opening the buried chest. He raised the lid.

Inside the box were a substantial number of bones including two skulls, one a child's. There were also two tablets similar to the one he had found below the ledge of Jesus, but twice the size. Wil reached for one tablet. He blew the dust from it as he held it up to the light. It said, *"My Beloved Wife is in Heaven with God."* He wasn't sure if he said it or thought it. Facts were coming so fast Wil could hardly grasp them. Wil set the first tablet down carefully and reached for the other. He read it out loud. *"Our Daughter, Our Love, is with God."*

His breath gone, Wil staggered back and sat on the stone table in the middle of the room.

He glanced at his watch. He had less than two minutes before he had to start his exit.

Wil again looked at the two inscriptions he had just found. A wife. A child. Why Jesus?

Wil went over the legend of Jesus' death and supposed resurrection again in his head. Everything had made so much sense until now. How does this tie in? Was Jesus buried in an occupied family tomb? The biblical account plainly states that Jesus had been put in a tomb where no one had ever been laid. Did this mean the whole tomb or only the designated ledge?

Wil looked at Jesus' ledge. "What does this all mean?" he whispered, looking for answers from the silent stones. He took his head in his hands and pushed on his brain as if to force an answer out.

How could he have missed this? The hurry and excitement? He felt like a detective who had failed to observe the obvious murder weapon coated in blood.

What did it all mean? He had to stay. But he couldn't. His

time was up. Wil put two bones, one of the wife and a smaller one belonging to the child, into his daypack. There wasn't room for the tablets or the skulls, the two items he really wanted to take. He hurriedly took down the curtains and used them as protection for the bones. He readied himself. When the light passed, he crawled and then ran as fast as he could to get to the wall. He only had seconds to get to the wall before Beth would start the last major diversion.

But before he made it to the wall, Beth screamed. It was troublesome that she was being so obvious. He was also upset she was early. But he didn't have time to debate her tactics. He continued running as fast as he could toward the wall and jumped to climb without checking if anyone was looking. He had to trust that Beth would hold up her end of the plan. He was smack on top of the wall when the light hit him. He looked like a kid climbing over a schoolyard wall who had just been caught by the principal. But it didn't matter. No one was watching.

The guards' verbal bantering had turned into something dangerous. Beth was trapped against the guardhouse, the shoulder of her dress pulled down. Two guards held her arms tightly against the wall. The guard between them flicked his cigarette away and began to caress her face. Terrified and helpless, Wil jumped off the wall and ran to the fence. He was under the fence and had it patched up in seconds, quicker than he had dreamed he could.

Wil pulled off his ski mask and put his sunglasses back on. He looked more like a dirty beatnik than a cat burglar. He unzipped his leather coat, dusted off his knees, and got into the light, but not so much as to be fully seen.

"Hey, woman! There you are!" Wil yelled at the top of his voice. The guards turned abruptly to stare at the unexpected intruder. Wil walked through the outer barrier made up of a four-guard audience. "Excuse me, guys." The guard preparing to kiss her backed off. Wil stepped into the center of the pack, firmly grabbed Beth's arm and jerked her free from the two holding her. They put up no resistance. "Thank goodness, they found you." The guards looked stunned.

"Thank you for catching her. I thought she'd gotten away." He gave her another jerk and tightened his grip. The guards understood this woman was his, and she was not going to get away again. He steered Beth in the direction of the parking lot.

Shocked by Wil's audacity, and perhaps shamed at having been caught, the guards didn't react.

Wil and Beth got into Beth's car. His legs felt like jelly as he stepped on the accelerator and drove away in an expeditious but controlled manner. When they had put some distance between themselves and their adventure, Wil glanced at Beth, who, with her head back and eyes closed, had not said a word since Wil whisked her away from the guards.

"I'm so sorry, Beth. That wasn't supposed to happen. Are you okay?"

"Thanks for getting there in time." Beth shivered. "I need a cigarette." She pulled a near-empty pack from her purse.

Wil chuckled. Nothing rattled Beth for long. "You know you ought to quit smoking those things. They're bad for you."

"Mmmm," she said as she took a puff, closed her eyes, and put her head back against the seat.

Being scientific

depends on who and why.

Chapter 30

WIL'S MISTAKE

Wil drove through the narrow streets and pondered the significance of what he had found.

"I was wrong. I should have waited," he murmured following a moment of excruciating silence. He was trying to formulate his thoughts. "I should have spent more time in the tomb before making the announcement. What have I done!"

They were still catching their breath. Beth glanced at him questioningly. He began to fill her in on his find. He spoke slowly, realizing that what he was confessing could not be absolved. Too much had happened because of his negligence. He wasn't sure what it all meant. There hadn't been time to assimilate the deluge of new information. Some things were obvious though, and one thing in particular. How could he have let this happen?

"Beth, I was wrong. I've made a terrible mistake."

"Oh?" All things considered, she thought their mission had been successful.

"I can't believe it!" His knuckles were white as he gripped the wheel.

"Dr. Wilson?"

Wil took another moment before responding. "Beth, I found more bones, a little girl's body and a woman. It was his wife, and – "

"Slow down, Dr. Wilson. You are going too fast. What do you mean – the bones of a little girl?"

Wil relaxed in the car seat, sat back and sighed. He knew he was going too fast. He started over.

"Beth, I found more bones – and more inscriptions."

"That's great!" Usually this would be considered fantastic news. Beth looked at Wil, who didn't seem happy. "Isn't it?"

"No, Beth, it isn't. Or at least . . . well, maybe it is. . . . Jeez! What have I done?" He let go of the steering wheel and shook his arms in the air, clenching his teeth.

"Slow down, Dr. Wilson!" said Beth, this time reminding him that they were traveling at forty kilometers per hour on a busy street. "And keep your hands on the wheel!"

Wil took a deep breath and let it out slowly. He was still organizing his thoughts. He said reluctantly, "Beth, the bones I found were not Jesus' bones."

He had her attention. Considering all that had happened, this was bigger news than when he first announced that he'd found the bones.

"I think the bones are those of a family. One was a little girl. Based on the inscription, she must have been the man's daughter. There were also bones of a woman. Based on the other inscription, they had to be those of the man's wife."

"What man?"

"Joseph of Arimathea . . . uh!" Wil grimaced, realizing he most likely was wrong again. "Of the guy in the tomb with Jesus – or who I thought was Jesus." None of his original conclusions now made sense.

"You mean it wasn't Joseph of Arimathea – and you really didn't find the bones of Jesus?" The synopsis stung.

"The bones I thought belonged to Jesus had to have been the older man's son's." Wil was still thinking out loud. "The man I thought was Joseph must have been the father." He paused before asking himself, "But how does '*The King of the Jews*' inscription tie in?"

"Couldn't they still be Jesus' bones?" asked Beth.

"No." He'd already worked that question through. "This was a family tomb. To suppose that I found the family tomb of Joseph, the Virgin Mary, Jesus and a mysterious sister of Jesus all in one place is ludicrous. And besides that, Jesus' family tomb would have been in Bethlehem."

The Bethlehem comment confused her, but he had answered her question.

Wil resumed his thoughts. It was silent in the car. Beth had seen Wil go into his thinking mode before and she knew it was best to let him be. Five minutes passed before he spoke again.

"Is Oskar Gunderson in town?" asked Wil. Dr. Gunderson was a colleague of Wil's at the Institute, an expert in archaeological genetics.

"I saw him yesterday in the lobby. I think so," said Beth. She had always thought Dr. Gunderson was such a nice man.

"Great." Wil began to show the resilience Beth so admired about her boss. "Get him to my office. Tell him I need to see him within the hour. Tell him it's really important!" They drove to Wil's house. Beth got out to walk around to the driver's side of the car as Wil said, "I'll meet you in my office in an hour. I have to do some things here before I head to the lab."

As Beth drove off to the Institute five minutes away, Wil was already in the house, headed toward his briefcase. He pulled out an eight- by ten-inch photograph of the tablet with the inscription "*The King of the Jews*," which he had thought belonged to Jesus. He also pulled out some papers that were the genetic screens done on the two sets of bones he had mistakenly thought were those of Jesus and Joseph of Arimathea.

183

He was mentally comparing the "*The King of the Jews*" tablet to the two tablets he had to leave behind in the tomb. "That's odd. It's only half the size." Wil was talking to his cat, Napoleon, who was rubbing around his legs wanting to get into Wil's lap. Wil was puzzled. "I don't understand."

Wil pulled out a videotaped copy of the dig when they had extricated the original two bodies. It seemed like an eternity ago. Sitting in his chair, remote in hand, Wil began to watch the video, which he hadn't viewed before. No need to. It was strange watching himself give orders to so many people in such a small place. "I was excited, wasn't I?" he said to Napoleon, who had finally reached his lap and snuggled in as if to watch the video as well.

A movement in the background caught Wil's eye. He hit rewind and then play. "What is that guy doing?" Napoleon meowed as Wil leaned forward. It was clear as crystal. The camera caught the action that, due to the angle, Wil could not have seen while in the tomb.

Wil rewound again and played it in slow motion. "He's picking something up and – " Wil stood abruptly, sending the cat flying. "The thief! He stuck it in his coat!" Wil was pointing at the screen with his right hand, his other hand pressed against his forehead.

Wil watched again as one of the helpers, the red-haired American kid supplied by the embassy, bent down near the collapsed wall, picked up a stone tablet, and put it under his coat. The kid stood up quickly as Wil ordered him to fetch the container for the "*The King of the Jews*" tablet he himself was holding. Wil noted how remarkably similar the tablet in his hands looked to the one the kid had hidden under his coat. Wil said to himself, "I can't believe it. The kid stole something from the tomb."

Wil ran a hand through his hair and began to pace. He had

caught the thief red-handed on tape. However, he was on the run from the U.S. government himself. If he told anyone related to the project, they'd likely be more interested in turning him in than in catching the thief. And it wouldn't make sense to go to the local authorities, who would probably do the same.

"If only I knew what that thief took. Maybe that would help resolve this mess." Wil grabbed his briefcase, made sure everything was there, and headed to his car. He only had a few minutes before meeting with Dr. Gunderson at the lab. Traffic was not bad and he made good time. Careening his car into his parking spot, he jumped out, hurried up the front stairs and down the hallway to his office.

"Hello, Oskar," said Wil to the kindly Dr. Gunderson pacing in Wil's office. Beth was pouring coffee. The sixty-year-old scientist turned and peered at Wil from under bushy eyebrows.

"This had better be good. You know, Wil, I do not get out of bed at five-thirty for just anybody." His eyes twinkled.

"I know," said Wil, taking a cup of coffee from Beth and handing it to his friend. Beth poured a second cup for Wil. "I need your help." He reached into his briefcase and brought out a report. "I suppose you've heard about my escapades in the States."

"Ja," said Dr. Gunderson, slipping into his German accent.

"Well." The story was much too long to tell. "I've gotten on the wrong side of some very important people. But it's worse than that. When I made the announcement about finding the bones of Jesus, I really thought I had."

"Thought you had?" Gunderson did a double take. "What do you mean?'"

"I found some other bones." Wil reached into his daypack that Beth had brought in from the car. "And I'm now convinced the bones I found were not the bones of Jesus or Joseph of Arimathea." Wil's face turned red.

"Whose are they?" asked the scientist, who was still puzzled about what any of this had to do with him. He added as an afterthought, "And where and when did you find them?"

"In the tomb about two hours ago," Wil said with a grin.

"What tomb?" asked his friend, logically not thinking it was the Garden Tomb since everyone in Jerusalem knew that site was permanently closed.

"The Garden Tomb – where I found the other bones."

Gunderson's coffee sloshed over the edge as his cup abruptly hit the saucer.

"Here's a copy of the forensic and genetic reports on the two sets of bones we originally discovered." Gunderson took the report from Wil.

"Here are bones from the two people I found in the tomb tonight." These Gunderson had more reservations about. He hesitated before accepting them.

"I need you to tell me if my theory is correct."

Beth was listening carefully. She hadn't yet heard the theory in its complete form.

After Wil laid out his thoughts regarding the bones, Gunderson asked, "Why don't you tell the authorities?"

"Who?"

"The people you have been working with the last few months."

"I can't."

"What do you mean, you can't?"

"Oskar, it's a long story . . . but I think they want to kill me."

"For bones?"

"No. They think I know something I'm not supposed to know."

"What is that?" The story was compounding.

"Oskar, you're going to have to trust me on this one. It's better if you don't know. But my biggest concern is the bones. I've turned the world upside down by announcing I found the bones of Jesus. The President has staked his re-election on my find. He can't afford the truth. Not now. This could ruin his chances for re-election since his main issue has become his 'Post-Christian Age' platform – which I hatched. I can only guess what measures they'll take to cover up this new discovery. I'm concerned that, if I don't act fast, they'll find the items I had to leave behind in the tomb and clean it all out before anyone has a clue. My mistake will become the truth for eternity."

Gunderson was beginning to catch on.

Wil went back to his theory regarding the bones, and asked, "Can you tell me if what we have is a family made up of a father, mother, son, and daughter?"

"I think so. But it will take some time." Oskar was pleased that what Wil was asking him to do was well within his capabilities.

"I don't *have* time, Oskar."

"I will see what I can do."

"Thanks. And Oskar, this has to be only between us."

At the door, Gunderson turned to Wil and Beth and sighed, "I have to say it, Beth. You look great in that dress." With that, he headed to his lab down the hall.

Wil sat at his desk. Beth leaned against the chair across from him, wanting to help. In the game of archaeology, which no one was better at than Wil, one of the biggest challenges was to put together a puzzle with only a few pieces. Wil had more than a few pieces. He had nearly all the pieces. He simply needed to put them together. But there was one piece that wouldn't fit no matter what he tried. It was the inscription on the first tablet: "*The King of the Jews.*"

He began to fumble with his briefcase. "I have to find the guy who took the tablet from the tomb."

Beth didn't know what Wil was talking about, but figured she would know soon enough.

187

Wil pulled out the planning documents of the early stages of the project. He remembered a memo that told the search team members where to meet prior to their midnight artifacts-recovery missions. He scanned the list of people who had received copies. Wil had met all of his team members, but was so focused on the mission that he hadn't paid attention to their names, particularly the guys who were coming along as packhorses. He wished he had.

"Beth, one of these people has the missing piece to the puzzle." Wil pointed to the list of thirty people. "I need to talk with that person. My problem is, if I guess wrong, I'm likely to give away that I'm back in Israel, and they'll catch me." He thought some more and handed her the memo. "Read the names to me and cross them out if I tell you to. Okay?"

Beth began to read the names on the distribution list, still unsure of what Wil meant by "the missing piece."

"Ahmad Mohammed?"

"No, he was Anglo."

"Steen Jorgensen?"

"Not him," said Wil. "I'm pretty sure he was the driver."

Beth read another name.

"Not her. It wasn't a woman. Cross off all the women." There were only two.

Beth began to read each name, one after the other. By the time she had reached the bottom of the list, all but two names had been crossed out. She showed the list to Wil.

"It's got to be one of them." Wil was closing in on his missing evidence. He opened his desk drawer and took out a phone book. "Let's see . . ." He began to thumb through the phone book and highlight the numbers he found. One of the names had two listings and the other had four. "Well, it's a start." He smiled.

Beth didn't like the way he looked at her.

"Beth, the guy was an American with red hair, glasses, and spoke with a southern accent. This is Jerusalem. What are the chances of there being more than one person in this city with one of these names matching that description?" He wasn't begging, but close. "I need you to call and try to figure out which one of these is the right guy."

"You know, Dr. Wilson," she said as she took the list, smiling but also partly serious. "I don't get paid enough for all this."

Wil agreed.

"I'll give it my best." Beth stood and went to her desk, where she dialed the first number.

A yawning "Howdy" came through the receiver. The drawl was so thick it was annoying. "This is Chris."

Beth's voice suppressed her excitement though her posture didn't. It appeared she might be having a lucky break.

"Hello . . . Chris," purred Beth. Her voice matched the red dress still hugging her body. "This is Sheila. I'm not sure if you remember me, but I was the girl in the cafe who made the comment about your beautiful red hair and glasses."

The other end of the phone was silent. Chris had no idea what Beth was talking about or why she was calling at seven-thirty in the morning. However, she apparently knew him, based on her accurate description, and he really liked the sound of her voice.

"Oh, yeah . . . I remember."

What a moron, Beth thought. But it was working.

"I was wondering if we might be able to get together some time." She breathed heavily.

"I just love men with red hair and glasses and, if you're interested . . . maybe we could . . ." She let the sentence hang.

"Wow! Really? Well I guess I could . . . When?"

Beth had him. "I've been up all night partying. Y'know what I mean?"

"Nooooo. Not a good girl like you." You could almost hear the guy's adrenaline pumping though his veins.

"I'm not good . . . and I *need* to see you right now. I mean *now!*" She was almost pleading. "I'll be there in thirty minutes. Where do you live?"

He was, without a doubt, an opportunist. He gave Beth directions. She smooched into the phone, teasing this guy who was now fully in rut, and hung up.

Beth ran into Wil's office. "Here's his address. I got him on the first call!"

Wil leaped up and walked in front of his desk. "You never cease to amaze me, Beth." And then, for the first time in their professional careers, he gave her a hug. It was a surprise to both, and Wil found himself apologizing.

Beth waved it off. "You'd better get going, Dr. Wilson. He's expecting a sexy girl named Sheila to show up at his door in thirty minutes. You don't quite fit the description, but I guarantee he isn't going anywhere."

"You're a remarkable woman," Wil said with admiration. He took the note and headed out the door.

Chapter 31

THE MISSING PIECE

Wil knocked on Chris's door. When the door opened, Wil was not sure if he was looking at the helper from the tomb or a red-haired, bespectacled John Travolta from *Saturday Night Fever*.

The shock on Chris's face was sincere. He thought he was going to get lucky, and here was the world-renowned archaeologist who had led the secret team at the Garden Tomb. Chris stepped back as Wil entered.

"We need to talk."

"But, I – "

"Nobody is coming, Chris. However, more than a beautiful girl named Sheila will be coming if I don't get what I'm looking for." Wil was pleased with how tough he sounded.

"But . . . ?" Chris was still in shock.

"Sit down and shut up." Chris sat, almost missing the chair. "I want the tablet."

"What tablet?" asked Chris, trying to look surprised. Wil had already seen Chris's look of surprise, and this wasn't it.

"The video caught you hiding the tablet under your coat. No one else knows about it. No one else will know about it – if you give it to me now. Where is it?"

Chris pointed toward his stereo system against the wall. The tablet was next to a Texas license plate, Mardi Gras beads, and a picture of Chris with the President's arm around him. They were standing in front of a banner that read, "University of Texas – Voice your Vote '96." It was his trophy case. This was a simple-minded young man.

"I didn't think anyone would miss it," he whined.

"Chris, that was really stupid!" Wil's tone turned paternal. He walked over and took the tablet that had been added to Chris's memorabilia. "Don't ever do anything like that again!"

Tears and fear covered Chris's face. Wil didn't sympathize. He turned and left the apartment, tablet in hand. He wanted to get out of there before his luck changed.

At his car Wil stopped to read the tablet. It was about the same size as the one that said, "*The King of the Jews*," which was indelibly imprinted in his mind. The rough edge at the bottom of this tablet matched the rough edge at the top of the first. There was no doubt. This was the other half of the tablet that started the juggernaut rolling. Wil studied the Aramaic inscription. It read, "*My son is in Paradise with*." Wil put the two pieces together in his mind. He staggered, steadying himself against the car, and muttered out loud, "*My son is in Paradise with the King of the Jews*."

Wil had the missing puzzle piece. His muscles rigid and his breathing strained, he persuaded himself to get in the car. He had to see what Gunderson had found out about the genetic comparisons.

He found Gunderson and Beth sitting in his office. They stood as Wil came in.

Dr. Gunderson spoke first. "Wil, the younger man is definitely the older man's son. The genetic screening report you gave me was conclusive on that. I am surprised no one else noticed."

This confirmed what Wil was thinking. "We weren't looking for it," admitted Wil. He knew that, had he been looking for all the facts, this whole mess could have been avoided. He had committed one of the most heinous, but all-too-common, errors in science. He had made his limited facts fit his expectations and desires.

"As for the woman, I can't quite prove it yet, but I'm certain she's the mother of the younger man and the little girl. It will take more time to be sure, but when you also consider who would normally be buried in a first-century Jewish family tomb, I would stake my reputation on it."

"Thank you, Oskar. I owe you a schnapps." Wil withheld his enthusiasm. He had the facts, but he hadn't solved anything. He needed to think. "If you don't mind, can I have a few minutes?" As Gunderson and Beth started to leave the room, Wil said, "Oskar, let me know if you find anything else."

Gunderson headed back to his lab but, before walking out the door, he fixed his twinkling eyes on Wil. "You sure got yourself into a fine kettle of bones now, Wil." Beth laughed. Wil felt sick. Gunderson left the room.

"That man sure does love his work doesn't he, Dr. Wilson?" Beth's eyes remained on the empty doorway. She walked toward the door. "I will be out here if you need me." She closed the door and sat at her desk in the office area, which also served as the greeting room for people waiting to see Wil.

After about thirty minutes of sitting at his desk in a near trance, Wil began to talk to himself.

"The father was a wealthy Jewish sympathizer of the Jesus movement. The child . . . no, the children . . . The family tomb . . . of course people would associate the empty tomb with the tomb of Christ."

The mumbling turned into an announcement. "It has to be the criminal from the cross! It has to be the repentant criminal from the cross!" Wil was now walking rapidly around the room, hands in the air, confident he had figured it out. "But what am

I going to do now?" He sat and pressed his palms to his eyes. He was in thought again. After a few moments he stood up straight and triumphant.

"BETH!" Wil shouted.

Beth quickly came into the office and Wil began to lay out his theory.

"Beth, I've figured it out. I didn't discover the tomb of Jesus. I discovered the tomb of one of the criminals – the one who converted – who died next to Jesus on the cross. The dating makes sense. The inscriptions make sense. Everything makes perfect sense."

"Uh huh," said Beth, realizing he would continue regardless of what she said.

"This tomb belonged to the father of the man who died on the cross next to Jesus. You know, the one the Bible says asked Jesus to remember him when Jesus came into his kingdom." Wil paused to catch his breath. "Do you remember what Jesus said to him?"

Beth opened her mouth to reply, but Wil continued. "He said, 'Today you will be with me in Paradise.' The inscription on the tablet makes sense."

Wil showed her the piece he had retrieved from Chris, and the photo of the half that was in the lab in the States.

"The little girl was the thief's sister, who must have died earlier, perhaps due to an illness. The woman, who also died earlier, was the mother. The man I mistakenly thought was Joseph of Arimathea was actually the father and husband. This was their family tomb. This poor chap lost his whole family before he died himself. Maybe the grief-stricken man even killed himself. After all, his son had just been disgracefully executed as a criminal. I don't know . . ."

Wil drew a hand across his forehead. "Whatever the case,

the bones I thought belonged to Jesus simply don't." He paused.

Beth took it in. It was incredibly logical, but there was one question that wouldn't go away. "What about the other chamber, the one tradition holds to be Jesus' tomb?"

Wil hadn't thought about that. It was a good question. He began to postulate out loud. "Well, for one thing, it is doubtful, based on first-century burial customs, that both chambers would have been in use at the same time. For all I know, it was never used." Wil caught himself. He needed to reserve the issue of the empty tomb for another day. The problem he had now was with the tomb that wasn't empty. He recouped his thoughts and got back on track.

Everything had fallen into place. "It's reasonable that the site became revered as a sacred Christian place. After all, the repentant criminal would have been the first Christian to die after Jesus' death. The fact that confusion arose over the ages is understandable considering how many times this area has changed hands. When the tomb was rediscovered in the nineteenth century, they made the mistake of thinking it was Jesus' tomb when, in fact, it was the tomb of the repentant man who had died next to Jesus on the cross." Wil collapsed into his chair. It had all sunk in. He looked imploringly at his friend. "Beth, what have I done?!"

Beth was silent. They both sat, thoughts turned inward, contemplating the repercussions of the two discoveries. What now?

Desperation destroys.

Chapter 32

KATHREEN

By the time Wil had finished filling in the details for Beth, it was nearly noon. He and Beth were hungry, exhausted, and needed a break.

"Beth, I think we'd better take a breather and get a little something to eat."

"I was hoping you would say that." Beth stood and stretched.

"You've been great." Wil sounded apologetic. He had the tenacity of a pit bull when he was onto something. Beth was used to it, but she was still only human.

"Let's take a break for a couple hours and meet back here at five o'clock. That will give me some time to figure out what I'm going to do and also allow me to stay out of the limelight. Perhaps Oskar will have come up with some more information by then."

Beth welcomed the break. "Sounds good. I have a few things to finish up. I will see you tonight."

Wil stuffed his papers into his briefcase and headed out the door. He left only the engraved tablet on his desk. Beth knew Wil had no intention of taking a break. At most, he would stop at a restaurant to eat while he continued to work, his papers spread out on the table. After that, he would head home to work some more, being careful to avoid people who might know him. At this point, only Beth, Dr. Gunderson, and poor, pathetic Chris knew Wil was back in Israel.

Close to an hour passed before three people walked in. Beth looked up to encounter the frosty gaze of a woman and two male companions. She had never met Kathreen Steele before, and the tone the three established made her apprehensive.

"Miss Beth Asmad?"

How did this woman know her name?

"We are looking for Dr. Wilson."

"He's not here, and I was about to leave." Beth did not like the looks of this.

"Why don't I take down your name and number and I will have Dr. Wilson give you a call when he gets back to Israel." It was a lie, but the feeling of apprehension wouldn't go away. She felt threatened.

Steele gestured to one of the men. Beth didn't have time to scream. Her head jerked back when the large hand was clamped over her mouth. They dragged her into Wil's office. In there screaming didn't matter. His office was separated from the hallway by Beth's, and no one would be able to hear her.

Steele walked behind Wil's desk, sat in his chair, and put her elbows on the desk with her hands clasped. Beth had been made to sit in a wooden chair directly in front of the desk.

Leaning forward so her chin was touching her fingers, Steele said, "Beth, let me be perfectly frank. We need some information. You are expendable. You can either tell us where Dr. Wilson is, or what you know," she paused. "Or you can suffer the consequences."

The situation reminded Beth too much of her childhood on the streets of Gaza. Hate and fear churned.

Steele was not in the mood for waiting, and her voice left no room to question what she meant. The President had been livid when he heard that Wil had disappeared. Steele knew her fate if she didn't find him. She had come to Jerusalem, after a day of fruitless searching in the States, when an airline's manifest indicated Wil had returned to Israel. Certainly he had made contact with Beth, and Steele wanted details.

"What is going on?" Beth was terrified. Her arms and back hurt from being shoved into the chair and having her hands tied behind her. "What did I do?"

Steele walked from behind the desk. The two men stood steady on either side of Beth.

"What do you want?" Tears were forming.

Steele was not going to waste time on this pawn. She was the first to hit Beth. She slapped her with her open hand so hard Beth's chair almost tipped over. "Where is Dr. Wilson? We know he has contacted you." Steele was bluffing, but Beth did not know that.

Before Beth could respond, one of the thugs punched her in the side below her breast. She was going to deny having been in touch with Wil, but the blow took her breath and she could only gasp for air.

"Let her talk." Steele told the thugs to back off. It wasn't because of Beth's tears.

Beth looked up. Her voice was halting. "I . . . do not know . . . what . . . you are talking about." She was having a difficult time breathing. "I . . .thought . . . he . . . was in the . . . States."

"Don't be stupid, missy. We're going to find out what you know. I don't want to have to kill you, *too*," she said with a grin. "Now where is the good doctor?"

That was apparently a cue for the men to hit Beth again. The first one punched her in the side of the head. Her ears rang. The other delivered a swift kick with his booted foot to her arm, which was twisted around the back of the chair. The crack of a bone was audible. Beth screamed. The pain was agonizing.

Another blow hit her face above her right eye. She almost passed out before Steele told them to back off again. It was hard to interrogate someone who was unconscious. Blood was dripping from Beth's lip, forehead, and arm.

Beth decided – *not another word*. She climbed into the shell she had developed as a Palestinian child on the streets of Gaza, and prepared herself for whatever came.

The beating went on for another fifteen minutes. A few blows, then a chance to speak. Still Beth said nothing. Eventually her tears stopped. Five more minutes. Then she passed out.

In frustration, Steele kicked the chair over. With a thud, the chair and Beth's unconscious body hit the floor. She was still tied to the chair, and a small pool of blood began to form beside her face.

"Great!" Steele began to pace around the room, her fists clenched and raised in front of her. "Now we can't learn anything from her!" It was her blow that had finally knocked Beth out. She was desperate. "Search their offices," she ordered the two goons.

"What are we looking for?" asked one of the men, not sure what their irate commander wanted him to find.

"Anything – notes, calendars, memos, addresses, directions. Something that will tell us where Wilson's gone."

One of the men sat in Wil's chair. He opened the desk drawer and began to read labels on files. Steele was searching the top of the desk. She couldn't find a clue. The other man was not having any luck at Beth's desk either.

In frustration, Steele stretched her arm out over the desk and wiped it clean with one sweep, sending everything flying across the office, including the stone tablet. Had she been more involved in the substance of the project, she would have thought more about this tablet that was almost identical to the one that had started this whole misadventure.

"Let's go. I want to get back to the embassy." They left the office. Beth was still unconscious. The pool of blood had grown.

Integrity is subordinate to truth.

Chapter 33

THE WAY OUT

Wil stood in his doorway and stared in disbelief at what had been his living room. His home was destroyed. Who had done this? What were they looking for? He walked to his desk and began to sit, realizing this might not be the safest place for him to be.

"Jeez – Napoleon!" The cat nearly caused a coronary when it jumped into Wil's lap even before Wil had hit the seat. He looked at his cat, realizing his only real family was also terrified. "It'll be all right," he said as he stroked Napoleon, who had curled up in his lap and begun to purr.

When Wil's heartbeat was restored, he said, "I gotta go." Wil picked the cat up and set him in the chair. "You stay here and keep an eye on the place. But stay out of the way." Wil turned to leave.

RING! The phone shrilled into the silence. Wil whirled and let out a scream, sending the cat streaking toward the closet.

Should he answer it? He let it ring a fourth time before picking up. He put the receiver to his ear and listened.

"Wil?" It was Gunderson.

"Yes." Relief was evident in Wil's voice.

"This is Oskar. I am in your office. It is Beth. She has been hurt. You had better get here quickly." Silence. "Wil?"

Wil was stunned. "Is she okay?"

"Wil, you need to get here quickly."

"I'm on my way."

The drive took longer than normal because of traffic. Why didn't he ask Oskar what had happened? What was wrong? Oskar had sounded so distraught.

Wil walked in to find Beth lying on the sofa, with Dr. Gunderson sponging her forehead and cheeks. The blood was still on the floor. Beth's face was swollen and her left arm was lying limp along her side.

"What happened? Did you call an ambulance?" Wil was pale.

"She would not let me." Gunderson shrugged in frustration.

"She wouldn't let you! What's going on?"

Beth spoke next. Her words were weak but clear. "Wil . . . a woman . . . Kathreen Steele – I think . . . two men . . . were looking for you. . . . I . . . did not tell them anything. I think . . . they want . . . to . . . kill you." The effort of speaking depleted her.

"I found her lying on the floor tied to a chair about ten minutes ago. She was just coming to. They apparently were looking for something." Gunderson gestured to the devastated office. "What is going on, Wil? Should we call the police?"

Wil went to Beth and gently touched her face, distressed. He smiled kindly and sat next to her in the chair Dr. Gunderson had vacated. Wil groaned as he looked at her, taking in the bruises and cuts.

"Wil?" The voice of compassion came from Beth. "What are we going to do?" He noticed the "we." Even now Beth was supporting him.

"How bad is it?"

"They broke my arm." She was ignoring the other injuries.

"Wil! What is going on?" Gunderson demanded to know the whole story. Wil knew he had the right to.

Wil gave him the two-minute version and then told him to take Beth to the hospital. They all agreed this should be kept quiet, at least for now. "I have some phone calls to make. You get her to the hospital. I'll figure this out. And Oskar – be careful."

They made a sling for Beth's arm with a spare shirt Wil kept in the office. With Dr. Gunderson's arm around her waist, Beth was able to walk. She winced with every step as they worked their way to Oskar's car.

Wil went to his desk and collapsed into his chair, lost in the deepest thoughts of his lifetime. His fear was now balanced with fury. The next step was clear. He put his briefcase on his desk and opened it, pulled out a dog-eared appointment book, and flipped to the phone numbers. He began to dial, but hung up before he had finished. It wouldn't be safe. He took his appointment book and jogged to the bank of pay phones outside the Institute's conference rooms and auditorium. There was no way they could monitor all these phones. He figured they had tapped Steve's home phone, but that didn't matter. It was nearly eight a.m. in D.C. and Steve would most likely be in his office at the church anyway. He hoped that wiretapping a church would have been a harder task. It rang three times.

"Good morning."

"Steve?"

"Yes."

"It's Wil."

"Wil! Is everything all right? What's going on? The FBI came by my office looking for you." Steve was anxious and unsettled.

"No." Wil paused. "Steve, everything is not all right. I need your help."

"What's wrong?" Steve asked.

Where to begin? There wasn't enough time to tell Steve everything.

"I need you to trust me."

"Of course!"

"I'm in trouble and I need you to do something for me."

"What is it?" Steve's anxiety had not subsided.

Wil was working up the courage to make his request.

"Wil?" said Steve to the uncomfortable silence.

"Steve, so much has happened. I can't explain it all now. I found some more bones." Wil took a breath and confessed, "I was wrong about the bones being the bones of Jesus." Steve was silent so long that Wil thought the connection was broken until he heard Steve catch his breath. "I also stumbled onto illegal activities involving the President. And now . . ." He swallowed. "They've beaten Beth and they want to kill me."

"What?" Wil could understand that Steve was having a hard time taking it all in.

"If I don't get your help, I'm sure they'll cover up the material I found and take me out of the picture and the whole mess I made will continue forever."

"What happened to Beth?"

"Some people working for the President beat her up in my office. They broke her arm, Steve. They were looking for me. Right now they don't know anything about the other bones I found. If we don't act now, I'm certain they'll find out and . . ." Wil exhaled. He knew he was right. "They'll kill me and my mistake will go on forever."

The scope of it all was overwhelming.

"What do you need me to do?"

"I need you to convince Congressman Jones to get on the next plane to Jerusalem with you. I need you to meet me at Cafe Hassan outside the north entrance to the Dome of the Rock by tomorrow at ten a.m. Israeli time."

"What!" Steve's volume caused Wil to pull the receiver a couple of inches away from his ear. "You're not serious!" After a space of silence, Steve said, "You're not kidding are you, Wil?"

"No. I have one chance for the truth to come out. I need you to be here. I need Congressman Jones. Please, Steve . . . trust me." Wil paused.

Wil took Steve's silence as agreement.

Steve knew Wil well enough to understand that he was serious and scared.

"Don't tell anyone, Steve. Get Congressman Jones on the next flight. Truth depends on it. Please, Steve. I have to go. Remember. Cafe Hassan, ten o'clock tomorrow morning." Wil hung up.

Wil took another deep breath, picked up the receiver, and dialed again.

"You have reached the office of Congressman Newcastle, your voice in Washington. If you are calling regarding a bill currently before the House, press one. If you are calling regarding the congressman's bid for the Senate, press two. If you are calling for any other reason, please stay on the line and someone will be with you in approximately two minutes. Thank you for calling Congressman Newcastle." Wil hated voice-messaging systems but figured this was the only way to get in touch with Hope without their call being monitored. Surely they wouldn't tap Congressman Newcastle's public relations line.

"Hello. Thank you for calling Congressman Newcastle. How may I help you?" It was a real voice. Sort of. It sounded like a Valley girl with political aspirations.

"I want to talk to Hope Fairview." This was not a request. It was a demand.

"Is there something I can help you with, sir?" The voice was both friendly and determined to screen the call in the manner she had been trained.

Wil was not going to deal with her. "Miss, I represent a

well-funded organization that has decided to shift our support from Senator Brown to Congressman Newcastle. I spoke yesterday with Miss Fairview, but I've lost her direct number. I've spent twenty minutes playing with this stupid voice messaging system and I am about ready to run out of patience. Tell Miss Fairview that, if she's still interested in our support, she'd better take this call now."

Wil's tone and the unusual request caught the young woman off guard. She didn't even bother to announce the call to Hope but, instead, put Wil directly through to Hope's extension.

"Hope?"

"Wil?" Hope sounded more relieved than curious. She was not expecting his call until that evening. She definitely didn't expect him to call her at work. And why did he call on this line?

"Hope, we don't have much time." Hope was unnerved with Wil's use of "we." He hadn't even thanked her yet for what she had done for him over the last thirty-six hours.

"I need you to do one more thing for me."

She couldn't miss Wil's urgency or sincerity. "What is it?"

"I need you to get Congressman Newcastle –"

"Congressman Newcastle!" Hope interrupted, hardly believing her ears.

"Yes, Congressman Newcastle." Wil didn't acknowledge her bewilderment. "I need you and the congressman to meet me at Cafe Hassan outside the north entrance to the Dome of the Rock in Jerusalem at ten a.m. tomorrow, Israeli time."

"What?" Hope was no longer calm. Now she was upset. She had gone above and beyond any call of duty or loyalty in helping out an old friend. She was probably a felon at this point. She was completely in the dark about what was going on, and now he was asking her to do the completely ridiculous. She regathered her composure. "You don't simply get a congressman on a plane and fly him to another country on thirty minutes' notice. Are you out of your mind?"

There was a moment of silence as Wil considered the merits of Hope's question.

"Hope, this is big. I already have Congressman Jones coming." Wil was bluffing and hoping at the same time. "And I need you and Congressman Newcastle to be here also."

This was the most peculiar thing Hope had ever heard. These two congressmen had been at each other's throats for twelve years. Was Wil trying to create another conflict in Israel to take the pressure off the peace process?

Hope's anger and frustration subsided as she again recognized the fear in Wil's voice. "Wil, what's going on?"

Wil realized he owed an explanation to Hope, who had probably saved his life less than two days ago even after he'd ignored her for nearly ten years. "Too much. I found more bones. The original bones are not the bones of Jesus. I was wrong." For some reason this was particularly hard for Wil to admit to Hope.

Silence. Hope's mind buzzed.

Ever since the press announcement about the bones two weeks ago, nothing transpired in Washington that didn't involve the bones – and the pending election. A handful of religious elected officials such as Congressman Jones, along with a couple of other representatives including Hope's Congress-man Newcastle, were still expressing some reservations. The pundits' speculations were that these few holdouts were doing so for political purposes. Following the President's and Senator Brown's taking up the banner to lead the country into the new 'Post-Christian Age,' nearly every politician of both parties had staked out a position on the bones. Except for the few holdouts, all had stated their belief that the bones were the bones of Jesus.

None were more adamant than the President or Senator Brown.

Congressman Newcastle's hesitation was thought to be related to timing and strategy. That was mostly true. He withheld judgment, not so much because he didn't accept the evidence, but because Brown had been so front and center in pontificating on the death of Christianity that Newcastle's gut told him to lie low on the issue, at least for a while. It seemed prudent to sit out the horse race while everyone else invested their reputations and careers on the bones of Jesus.

Ironically, Newcastle's reluctance confounded the press and Congressman Jones. Jones and Newcastle were never on the same side of anything. At times it appeared that one would take a position only after the other took a stand. However, it became clear that Congressman Jones's zeal on this issue was completely unrelated to Newcastle. Rather, Jones was determined to expose what he sincerely believed was a major violation of the separation of church and state as well as a misuse of governmental powers.

"I've also come across some information confirming illegal activity by the President." Wil paused. He knew it was too much information. "They're going to kill me, Hope. They've already beaten up my secretary, Beth."

"Kill you?" Hope tried to keep her voice from rising as others in the office glanced her way.

"Some people from the President came here looking for me and they beat up Beth. Hope . . . they broke her arm."

Hope let this sink in. "Why do you need the congressman?"

"Because I have reason to believe they will cover up my new findings. I had to leave them in the tomb and they don't know about them yet. If they did . . ." Wil let the obvious fade away. "Plus, I need his credibility. If I show up in public, it'll be over. I can't do this by myself."

"Why not?" Hope's reporter past was coming out. Even as she asked her question, she knew the answer was that such an announcement would be a political deathblow to too many people who would have to admit they were wrong. The two most vulnerable were the President and Senator Brown. Their reversal could do nothing but destroy any chances of re-election. This was even before Hope learned about the payroll diversions to the President's re-election campaign.

Wil answered Hope's question anyway. "Because they will not reverse themselves. It's clear to me that the President is calling the shots and he can't afford any more surprises. He told me that himself. The President and the Israelis will lie to prevent the truth coming out, just like they did when I found the first bones." Wil paused.

"And politicians have too much to lose if they tell the truth." He knew he was running out of time. He took a deep breath and asked with finality, "Are you coming or not?"

He waited.

"Hope?"

More silence.

"We'll be there." Hope put more conviction in her voice than she felt.

"Good. I'll see you in fifteen hours – ten a.m. Cafe Hassan. Don't say anything to anybody," Wil commanded as he hung up.

Hope put down the phone, mildly insulted that Wil had added the last line. Of course she wouldn't tell anybody. The stakes were clear to her, but she couldn't suppress her reporter's instincts as they began to surface in full force. She picked up the phone again to call an old friend.

The call was answered after one ring. "Barry Rosen."

"Barry, it's Hope. How quickly can you have your camera to the airport?"

"Well, it depends. Do I go with the camera, or does it go by itself?" Barry joked.

She laughed with her old friend. "You jerk! Of course you can come with the camera!"

"Why, what's up?"

Hope didn't answer. Instead, she instructed him to get himself, his passport, and his camera to Dulles without anyone knowing. He had forty-five minutes. After further instructions as to where to meet, she ended the conversation with, "You'll have the film of your life."

Hope took a moment to drum up her courage, then walked into the congressman's office.

Wil's next call was to Dr. Ibriham Moshen, the archaeologist he had drafted into the search for the bombs prior to the Secretary of State's visit. Wil filled him in on the whole situation. Not only was his friend shocked at the news, he was furious that they had hurt Beth. He was still angry with the way he had been treated when the advance team was disbanded and with how the whole explosives story was covered in the news. He was the one who had found the explosives at the Church of the Holy Sepulchre and they never once mentioned anything about it. All the focus had been on the Garden Tomb.

Dr. Moshen said he didn't need to know everything. He was simply ready to help.

Wil had one more call to make. This one was the most risky but he had to make it. He began to dial. Before he finished, he set the receiver back on the hook. He stood up, squeezed out of the phone booth that had temporarily served as his office, and headed into the darkening streets of Jerusalem.

Chapter 34

THE COLONEL

Colonel Rabin opened the door as his children crowded around his legs and his wife called, "Who is it?" from the other room. His tie was off and his shirt collar open. He had only recently gotten home from work.

"Dr. Wilson, what a nice surprise," he said, sincerely meaning it. "Please, come in."

Wil smiled lopsidedly and shook the colonel's extended hand as he entered the room. More privacy seemed necessary. "Can we be alone?"

With a gesture of his hand, Rabin cleared the room. The children scampered to other parts of the house. He gestured for Wil to have a seat. "What can I do for you?"

After settling himself on the sofa, Wil faced the colonel. "I've made a terrible mistake."

Rabin looked at Wil and waited.

Wil shook his head and sighed. This would be about the fifth time tonight he had explained the situation. "I found some more bones – "

"That is nice," responded Colonel Rabin not sure why this would bring the famous archaeologist to his door.

"– in the Garden Tomb."

Rabin sat up. "But how did you get in?" He was well aware of the security measures put in place following the find. No one had been in the tomb since the night they had sent the bones to the lab in the States. The fences went up immediately, and guards were posted continuously.

"I crawled." Wil said with a grin. But he wanted to get on with the more important issues. Clearing his throat he said, "The bones we – you and I – discovered were not the bones of Jesus."

"Oh?"

"They were not Jesus' bones." Wil repeated. He knew that, if Colonel Rabin really heard what he was saying, he would know what that meant.

Rabin nodded. He was well aware of the implications. He knew about the chaos their find had caused in the U.S. and among Christians around the world. He had also noticed the spin the Israeli government had put on it as they began to reach out to their brothers in the Judeo (no longer Judeo-Christian) tradition, hoping to again bolster the pre-eminence of Judaism. "But why are you talking to me?"

"I need your help. We have to get back into the tomb before they scrape it clean . . . cover it up . . . destroy the evidence."

"Do they know you got into the tomb and found more bones?" asked the colonel, not bothering to question who "they" were.

"No. I haven't told them. It's more complicated than that."

"Tell me."

"The discovery of the new bones is news the President will not want to hear. It would destroy his re-election hopes. I've also, accidentally, come across some information regarding illegal activity by the President. The FBI, and likely others, are looking for me. They beat up my secretary. They destroyed my home. My life is in danger."

"Slow down, Dr. Wilson," the seasoned colonel encouraged the man he had grown to respect.

"Okay." Wil gathered his thoughts and started over. "I was already in trouble before I found the new bones. I had come across some correspondence substantiating criminal activity by the President. They were already monitoring me and I was beginning to believe my life was in danger." Wil sighed. "Believe it or not, I was worried that I would never be able to get back into the tomb and complete my research. I knew they were going to take me off the project and I had to get back into the tomb at least one more time." Wil thought about what he had said. "Perhaps I'm crazy to be so concerned about finishing my work even as people want to kill me . . ."

The colonel moved his head in agreement.

"I simply didn't know what to do. I decided to break into the tomb to have one last look. So there I was, playing spy and sneaking into the Garden Tomb, and what do I find? More bones. I found more bones! They were the bones of the mother and sister of the man I thought was Jesus. It turns out the older man was the father. The father-son relationship has been confirmed by DNA analysis. It wasn't Jesus. The President of the United States has staked his re-election hopes on championing a new world order built on the fact that the resurrection did not happen. He has been adamant that America needs to be freed from what he has called 'the restrictive Christian myths and traditions.' He obviously can't reverse himself now." Wil ran his hands through his hair.

"So why not go to the Israeli authorities?" Asked the colonel, even though he suspected such an act would be futile.

"I've thought about that. It also worries me. Based on what I've seen on this project, the Israeli government has no choice but to go along with the President. That is," Wil allowed, "if they didn't want to keep it silent for their own reasons. It's apparent that Senator Brown, who heads the Foreign Relations

Committee of the Senate, will stop all funding to Israel if they do not play with the President. The elections are now two weeks away. For the President to have to reverse himself on this issue would destroy his chances of re-election. I know they'll bury my find and continue on the course I so ignorantly set for them a few weeks ago."

The colonel was convinced. He was experienced enough to know the merits of what Wil was saying, and nodded his understanding.

"I've really made a mess of it," Wil said.

"But, Dr. Wilson, my good friend, what can I do?" Rabin asked.

Wil looked up. "I believe my only chance is to expose it all. If I don't, once they find out about my latest discovery, it's obvious they'll kill me and bury the facts forever. We have to get back into the tomb and retrieve the artifacts I had to leave behind." Wil took a breath. "And, believe it or not Jakob . . ." Wil called him by his given name for the first time. "While I want the truth to be made known, I also wouldn't mind continuing to live."

"Why did you come to me?" Rabin was now fully on board with Wil's situation. He moved to tactics.

"Because we're going back to the tomb in thirteen hours and I need your help to get in."

"Ah."

"I need you to arrest me and take me into your headquarters."

"What are you talking about?"

"I have a plan for some people to re-enter the tomb and expose the truth of what I found."

"And how are they going to do that, especially if you are under arrest?" asked the colonel. He had justifiable doubts.

"Do you really want to know?" asked Wil, trying to provide cover for the colonel to plead ignorance.

Rabin, picking up on Wil's nuance, went back to the original request. "Okay, so why do you want me to arrest you?"

"For one thing, I think I stand a better chance of staying alive if you're near me. For another, it will provide a diversion to allow my team to get into the tomb."

Sitting back in his chair, eyes locked with Wil's, the colonel sighed. "Okay, let us figure out how we are going to do this."

They discussed strategy for the better part of two hours. It was nearly midnight when Wil said, "I'd better be going."

"Where? I thought you said your house was destroyed."

"It's still there . . . but I guess you're right – that might not be the best place to go. I just need to get lost until tomorrow morning."

Colonel Rabin could see how tired Wil looked, his face pale and his eyes puffy. "That is fine. But first you will eat something and then take a little rest – here." He called for his wife.

The colonel woke Wil at five a.m. "You had better get going before it gets light outside. Here is some breakfast. Take it and go."

Wil got up, took the food, expressed his appreciation, and left the house, hoping to stay lost until the ten o'clock meeting.

Two hours later, the colonel left for work. As expected, there was a warrant for Wil's arrest as a fugitive from the American government.

Whether someone is an ally or an enemy is often contingent on the third player.

Chapter 35

THE TEAM

Other than Dr. Moshen, who arrived about three minutes late, and Beth, everyone was at the Cafe Hassan precisely at ten o'clock. Beth's cast and her badly bruised and swollen face disqualified her from the role she had been going to play. Gunderson and Wil were not going to let her take any more risks, no matter how much she insisted. Gunderson's job was to keep her safe at his house. This meant Wil was going to have to persuade Hope to be the decoy. He wasn't sure how easy that was going to be considering the last role he'd had her play.

Wil's face was haggard and his eyes red. He was two days overdue for a shave. Those who had traveled all night didn't look much better, except Hope, who looked great. Apprehension filled the air. Wil was surprised to see the cameraman at the table, but readily acknowledged Hope's wisdom in bringing Barry along. Small talk was at a minimum as they all sat around a circular table in the back of the cafe drinking thick black coffee, not so much for the pleasure as for the caffeine.

Wil began the meeting. "Thank you for coming. Let me explain what I need you to do. In about two hours I'm going to be arrested by a friend. This should provide a distraction, since the authorities will hopefully be so focused on me that you can proceed to the tomb." Wil did not waste any time in rolling out his plan. In his single-mindedness he had not fully appreciated the troubles the rest of them had encountered. It was rather presumptuous. These people, for some reason, were willing to put themselves in harm's way for him even though all of them had plenty of reasons not to do what they were about to do.

Wil continued, "My good friend, Dr. Ibriham Moshen," he nodded in his direction, "is going to lead the team. Hope will need to act as a decoy to distract the guards. I need you," looking directly at Steve, "to stand guard and be prepared to intervene, if needed, to assist Hope if she gets into any trouble. When Beth and I did this two nights ago, things almost got out of control." Bewilderment and concern registered on the faces of Hope and Steve. "I would like –"

Congressman Jones could not stand it anymore. In his soft, southern accent he began to speak for the rest of the group. "Dr. Wilson, we realize we are sitting on a time bomb. It also is obvious that all of us around this table are prepared to have our derrières blown off when this sucker explodes. However, please do us the courtesy of filling us in a little more. As Congressman Newcastle and I discovered on our rather unannounced detours from Washington to this dirty little cafe in the center of a country where we are not supposed to be, you did not exactly provide complete information to your convincing henchmen." He smiled at Hope and Steve.

Wil's face revealed embarrassment and contrition. He knew he owed them, and the world, an apology. Had he not jumped the gun with his announcement, he might have been allowed to get back into the tomb and discover the other bones. He wasn't sure of that, but he did know he had made a tremendous mistake. Wil sat down at the table with the group, putting off his professorial demeanor.

"You're right. I'm sorry." He looked down. "I realize this whole mess is my fault. I was wrong about the first set of bones.

I sincerely appreciate that you're willing to trust me after all the trouble I've caused." He gave a cathartic sigh and met their eyes. "But this out-of-control train has taken on a life of its own, and I'm convinced the only way to stop it is by getting everything out in the open. I've thought about simply going to the press, but I don't think they would believe me – especially after the President's spin-doctors got to them. I've thought about asking one of you to make an announcement, but I lack the evidence, such as the new tablets or the memo regarding the President's illegal payroll diversions. They would merely cover everything up."

"Payroll diversions?" asked Congressmen Jones and Newcastle simultaneously.

"I'll explain in a minute. I've also thought about having someone like Ibriham go public with the other bones I've found, but the tablets, the bones, the skulls – all the evidence is still in the tomb. We have to get to it before they find out about it." He took a deep breath. "I really believe the only chance is to do what I have planned. Besides, if we don't do it soon, I will probably be dead and I won't be around to help rectify this terrible mess I've made."

The group was silent for a few moments. Wil prepared to start over, this time from the beginning, more slowly and in more detail.

He took about thirty minutes to explain the whole situation: the invitation to be on the advance team before the Secretary of State's visit; the night of the find; the explosives cover-up; the death of the fanatic from the tomb; his announcement; the "Post-Christian Age" platform; the President's threats; Brock; the phone records; the payroll diversions to the President's re-election campaign; his escape; the second find; concerns about Senator Brown forcing Israel to stay in line with the President;

the beating of Beth; Colonel Rabin's support. He painted the picture more slowly and deliberately than he had ever done, even for himself. The group was intensely focused on his words, which were spoken in near whispers. They nearly jumped out of their chairs when the waiter offered them more coffee. They all declined in a babble of "No, thank yous."

The outcome of Wil's explanation was a deepening of purpose – of mission – by all involved, including Wil. They were going to see this thing through. They were not congressmen or scholars or pastors or reporters anymore. They were crusaders. They had moved beyond a concern for Wil's or, for that matter, their own safety. Their faces registered shock, disgust and anger. They were determined this abomination would end. So be it!

"I've always known our government might be involved in this kind of shenanigans," Congressman Newcastle said to Congressman Jones as they left the table. Newcastle and Jones had changed from adversaries to comrades, courtesy of this high-risk collaboration. Newcastle continued, "But for some reason, I've always thought it was for some greater good. This is sickening. The world has been turned upside down and perhaps the greatest cover-up of all time is going on, and is likely to continue. And for what – the job security of a few despicable, degenerate pigs." Jones nodded as Newcastle added, "I'm looking forward to seeing these jerks fry." Hope raised her eyebrows and smiled. These were strong words for the normally mild-mannered gentleman.

Congressman Jones commented that Wil had forgotten to mention the separation-of-church-and-state issue he had been so worked up about for the last few weeks. "But," acknowledged the congressman, "there are some bigger issues at hand." He looked at Congressman Newcastle with a smile. "We'll take that up another day. Today, we have a perversion of truth and justice to return to the mire from which its makers crawled!"

For Steve and Congressman Jones, this was the first time in the past month they were not having to deal with the reality that their religion was dead.

Wil instructed them to start precisely at two p.m. He hoped that his capture would be well enough known by then to distract the people looking for him and also to keep attention off the tomb.

Steve was the last to leave the table before the group set out to prepare for their mission. He put his hand on Wil's shoulder and, with the assurance only a pastor and lifelong friend was capable of giving, told Wil, "Everything's going to work out." For the first time in two weeks Wil believed it would.

Times to act happen.

Chapter 36

THE STRIKE

Exactly at noon, thirty minutes after the others had left, Colonel Rabin and one of his men stopped for coffee at Cafe Hassan. After a brief performance between the colonel and his subordinate, who not very discreetly pointed Wil out, Colonel Rabin announced himself in a voice loud enough for everyone in the cafe to hear.

"Dr. Wilson, I need to take you into custody." Wil stood up as if complying. With everyone watching, he tried to make a break for it. To no avail. The colonel's subordinate caught him, threw him to the ground, and handcuffed him. This was how they had planned it, but Wil hadn't foreseen the hardness of the floor or the discomfort of having his hands jerked behind him for the handcuffs to be applied. He also had never tried to get off a floor with his hands tied behind his back. Rabin helped pull Wil to his knees. It hurt.

"I'm sorry folks," said the colonel. "Please go back to your coffee." Wil was helped to his feet and they walked out, Rabin grasping Wil's upper left arm.

The colonel took Wil to his headquarters and sat him next to his desk, still in handcuffs, then went to have a conversation with his superior. They returned together to retrieve Wil. Rabin frowned. They had received orders to transport Wil to the American Embassy. This was not according to plan.

The three rode in silence, Rabin and Wil making uneasy eye contact. Wil was waiting for some kind of signal or clue from his friend. None came. His anxiety increased.

At the embassy, the colonel and his superior were thanked and summarily dismissed. It was only by chance that Rabin caught a glimpse of Steele as she opened an office door at the end of the hallway. He saw her walk in the direction they had taken Wil. She was accompanied by two large men in civilian clothes. Rabin narrowed his eyes in suspicion. He concealed his thoughts and his feelings of helplessness while heading back to headquarters.

While Wil was explaining to the ambassador why he had left the U.S. without telling anyone, Steele walked in. "Why, Dr. Wilson," Steele began with an icy smile. "You've had us all so concerned since your unannounced departure. It seems that some people in Washington are very worried about you. What were you planning to do in Israel *this* time?"

"I live here. I work here. What do you mean?" responded Wil, trying to stall.

"It seems your departure made the President himself nervous enough that I've been asked to monitor your behavior. Now, why is that do you suppose?"

Wil ignored Steele and turned back to the ambassador. He hoped the ambassador would intervene on his behalf. Wil found it ironic they were in the same room in which it all began about two months ago. Surely the ambassador would see through Steele and bring this to an end. Or was he involved also?

"Why have I been brought here? Does the United States government need my help on another project? Is the Secretary coming back?"

The ambassador shrugged somewhat helplessly. He was still in the dark about what was going on.

Steele hated being slighted and had no problem seeing through Wil's veneer of ignorance. "Very cute, Dr. Wilson. Why don't you kindly tell us what you've been up to for the last forty-eight hours? You've had a lot of very important people concerned."

Wil's look of ignorance fooled no one. "Have I done something wrong?"

"Wrong?" mocked Steele. "Now, why would you ask that? Why would *we* be concerned with the sudden disappearance of Mr. Let-me-turn-the-world-upside-down-without-telling-anyone?" Her voice had turned venomous. "You, Dr. Wilson, are a troublemaker, and perhaps even a traitor. Your violation of agreements has created a lot of concern."

Wil ignored the name-calling. He felt bad, but not because of any discomfort he had caused this witch or her boss. "Why am I being held here? I demand to know. Tell me – what have I done?" Wil was trying to make as much fuss as he could. He turned back to the ambassador. "I want to see an attorney," Wil demanded, knowing he wouldn't get a response.

The ambassador felt extremely uncomfortable with the whole way this situation was being handled. What was the big deal? Dr. Wilson was an archaeologist. A "traitor"? What could he possibly know? And you can't treat people the way this woman does. He thought it merited a call to D.C. to see if there was more to it. Besides that, Steele was starting to get on his nerves. Not bothering to excuse himself, he left the room. Steele locked the door.

Wil was now alone with Steele and her two thugs and he didn't like it. He had concluded that at least Steele didn't know about his recent discovery at the tomb. So far, that part of his plan was working. He had total confidence in the people he had shared coffee with that morning. He looked at the clock above the refreshment bar at the end of the room. If he could keep Steele distracted for another hour or so, he calculated, everything would work out fine. His big concern was the next thirty minutes.

One of Steele's assistants sneered like a playground bully looking for the next little kid to beat up. He kept rubbing his right fist with his left hand. The other opened a black briefcase and began to take out objects that looked like tools used by a dentist.

Wil knew his strengths. Endurance of pain was not one of them. He'd had plenty of it as a kid, but that was a long time ago. He knew they could eventually get him to say whatever they wanted with only one of those shiny tools. He had to stall. But how long he could make it last he didn't know. He hadn't counted on out-and-out torture. This was the United States Embassy for heaven's sake!

Wil decided to go for the direct approach. He would tell part of the truth and then try to negotiate a workable solution. Something like, "I promise not to tell anyone, if you promise not to kill me." It was a long shot, but he thought it might buy some time. He also hoped that, if they were negotiating with him, they might not torture him. He had temporarily forgotten what shape they had left Beth in.

"Is this about the payroll diversions?" he asked.

Satisfaction spread over Steele's face. It was too easy. She expected the scientist would have required at least a little help to convince him to tell her whatever he knew. "What do you know about payroll diversions?" She motioned for the two men to relax.

"That you . . ." Wil was trying to come up with something other than the truth, but he couldn't. "You were funneling money through The Bones Project to the President's re-election campaign." Wil began to think he had given up too quickly. Now he had no choice but to continue. He told the whole story about sneaking into the office and finding the memo. He was adding many more details than his audience wanted, but he was trying to buy time and at least they hadn't hurt him yet.

While Steele was pleased to get to this point, she was still not relaxed, and she was tiring of the unnecessary details. She needed more and skipped to the bottom line. "What proof do you have, and have you told anyone?" Steele was hoping it all would be as easy as the first part.

Wil began, "I have – " and then caught himself. She didn't know whether he had a copy of the memo or if he had told anyone! Wil almost wanted to thank her for the plan she had unintentionally given him, but he was too busy trying to come up with the rest of the story. He started with a demand. He figured he was in as good a negotiating position as he could hope for. "I'm not going to tell you until I get some guarantees of my own." He tried to sound tough, but it came across like a plea.

"What kind of guarantees?" asked Steele. She walked over to the table in the corner of the room and poured a mug of coffee.

Wil was working on his next line as she walked up to him. taking a sip from her mug. It was his turn in the negotiations he had started.

Before he could respond, Steele took the large mug from her lips and threw its steaming contents into Wil's lap.

"Do you really think you are in a position to ask for anything?"

Wil opened his mouth to cry out in pain, but nothing came. A powerful hand clamped over his mouth and nose and he felt a searing jab to his lower rib cage. He hadn't been hit like that since his childhood. He was convinced a rib was broken. Bent double and struggling for breath, he knew he had to talk, but he could not. Where the heck was the ambassador? Was he going to come back?

"Listen here, Dr. Wilson. You *are* going to answer my questions and you had better come clean pretty quick. Otherwise, they'll be taking you out of this room in pieces."

The goon removed his hand as Wil gasped for breath. He knew his only hope was to start over.

"I know about the payroll diversions." He then began to spin a long and detailed lie about notes and lock boxes and other hiding places for the copies he had made of the memo. Steele would have interrupted him, but his list of places detailing where he had stored the information was so plausible she thought he was telling the truth. She eventually gave him a pad of paper and told him to start writing. She needed this list so she could dispatch people to retrieve and destroy the evidence Wil had dispersed all over D.C. and Israel.

As bad as his situation looked, Wil's tactic was working. Other than an occasional kick or punch because he wasn't writing fast enough, Wil wasn't experiencing the complete agony he had been dreading. And Steele appeared a little less tense. She had contained her enemy and, at least for now, she thought things were headed in the direction she wanted.

While Wil was struggling to keep Steele occupied and himself alive, Hope, Steve, the two congressmen, Moshen, and the cameraman readied for the break-in.

Hope casually strolled toward the guards. As she subtly drew their attention, she gently squeezed the button in her pocket, which caused a car in the parking lot to burst into flames. Beth had wanted a new car for quite a while. After Wil assured her he would buy her a new one, she reluctantly agreed to go along with the part of the plan that called for the destruction of her car.

Hope became hysterical, screaming that her car was on fire and someone was trying to kill her. Steve stood back, but close enough so that Hope knew he was there. As the guards left their posts, the rest of the team stepped up to the gate.

"I've always wanted to do this," drawled Congressman Jones as he cut the chain that held the gate to the post. Congressman Newcastle pushed the gate and held it open for Moshen, who went through with his bag of instruments. Newcastle turned to his fellow commando congressman. "After you." Barry followed them. They were through the gate in ten seconds. The team, led by Moshen, headed for the tomb.

The camera was rolling as they set the lights in place. Moshen began narrating into Barry's CNN camera. As he removed the two tablets from the bones box, he read them for the camera. He then put them into a carrying case they had brought along. He did the same with the skulls and a few other artifacts. It was much faster than any scientist liked to work, but he didn't have much time. Jones and Newcastle looked on in gratified amazement. They had finally realized what they were doing and that it wasn't a dream.

By the time the press, along with other cameras, showed up to take photos of Beth's burning car, enough people had gathered in the area that the guards would not have risked shooting anyone. The team had been in the tomb for thirty minutes before the guards noticed movement inside. It didn't take them long to apprehend the peaceful trespassers along with their two accomplices, Hope and Steve.

The guards contained them in an area near the front gate. The lieutenant in charge was just setting down the receiver when Colonel Rabin, whom none of Wil's group had met, showed up with a security detachment. The lieutenant had called headquarters to inform them of what had transpired and who his notable prisoners were. Colonel Rabin informed the lieutenant that he had been dispatched to take the group, along with Barry's camera and film and the artifacts Dr. Moshen had retrieved. The lieutenant was not willing to question his superior, though he was surprised at how quickly the colonel and his detachment had made it to the scene.

Colonel Rabin ordered that the gate be secured with some of his own troops to supplement the embarrassed guards. "Anyone who tries to get into the tomb *is to be shot. Is that understood?*" He stated this loudly enough for the onlookers to hear.

The congressmen protested their treatment and declared diplomatic immunity. They even sought help from the shocked press gathered around the group as they were ushered to the colonel's van and loaded with the help of a couple of the colonel's men. Once in the van, the captives continued to protest. Colonel Rabin spoke above their protests.

"I am sorry Congressmen Jones and Congressman Newcastle. I had to do it this way. Wil is in trouble and I thought this was the only way to solve the problem."

He had their attention.

"Miss, does that cell phone work?" The colonel gestured toward Hope.

Hope nodded hesitantly.

"Call your friends at the press and have them meet us at the American Embassy. Please do it now." His tone of voice got an immediate response as Hope began to dial. The call probably wasn't necessary since the van was leading a parade of press vehicles through Jerusalem.

As the van approached the gate, the guard recognized Colonel Rabin from earlier that day when he had delivered Wil. The announcement that he had two United States congressmen with him assured his passage. The van passed through the gate, as did more press than the Marine gatekeepers could control. The group followed the colonel as he led them up the front stairs of the embassy and into the foyer, where they demanded to see the ambassador.

Seconds later, Ambassador Worthington hurried in. He had left Steele and Wil roughly an hour before. An unexpected meeting with one of his senior staff prevented him from making it to his office where he had planned to make his phone call to D.C. The congressmen took over the introductions and logistics and demanded to see Wil, who they knew was "being held against his will and without proper representation."

Worthington was stuttering from surprise and shock. He couldn't quite grasp what was happening. It was difficult for him to comprehend how these two congressmen could be on the same side of anything. And what were they doing in Israel? A quick-thinking aide whispered in his ear, "Do it. It's your only chance to get out of this clean."

The ambassador turned to the two guards standing by his side. "Get Dr. Wilson – now!"

A tense minute passed as they disappeared down the hallway. When Wil was produced, the two Marines, their weapons sheathed, tightly escorted him. As they approached the crowd, one of the Marines was giving instructions on his shoulder-mounted radio. "Take the two men in the east-wing conference room into custody." Wil held his side as he walked unsteadily toward the group, his lip bleeding. The ambassador was shocked. What had happened?

Steele was pulling on the Marines, attempting to stop them. "Don't! I'm ordering you to stop! On the authority of the President, I am ordering you to take him back to the room." She began to jerk on one of Wil's arms, causing him to wince and gasp in pain until a Marine pulled her off. Then Steele noticed the crowd. Panic. Control. She walked ahead of Wil and the Marines, directly to the ambassador. "Mr. Ambassador, on the authority of the President, do not do this. Dr. Wilson is not to be released." The ambassador ignored her.

"Mr. Ambassador, I am ordering –"

"Shut up, Kathreen." He had put up with her long enough and, after seeing Wil's condition, he was determined to distance himself from this woman and whatever she was involved in. He turned to one of the guards. "Will someone please remove her?"

A Marine stepped forward and began to escort her away. Steele struggled with him while yelling at the ambassador, "I'm warning you!"

Her words were disregarded. The Marine attempted to politely, but firmly, remove her from the scene.

Steele gave up on the ambassador and directed her commands to Wil. "Dr. Wilson – do not say anything!"

Wil didn't even acknowledge her.

"Dr. Wilson!" Steele was out of control. She grabbed her Marine escort's gun and started running at Wil, screaming and pointing the gun in his direction. It was doubtful she knew how to use it, but the onlookers screamed and ran for cover or dropped to the ground. That is, except for the ambassador, who stood perfectly still, his eyes wide in disbelief. A few cameramen, nerves toughened by experience, caught the whole episode on film. A quick-thinking Marine tackled Steele and took the gun away as she continued to scream and kick.

"Get her out of here." The ambassador had had it. He still wasn't sure what was going on, but Steele was unquestionably over the edge.

The crowd of staffers and reporters began to get to their feet and refocus on Wil. As the Marines were dragging Steele away, the watchers could hear her yell her final spin on the situation.

"The President didn't know anything about this. The diversions were all my idea. The President didn't . . ."

The press appreciated the lead, though they were not sure what she was talking about.

After a few handshakes and hugs, Wil stepped up to the crowd of reporters and cameras gathered in front of the embassy. The two congressmen and Dr. Moshen laid some packages in front of Wil.

Congressman Newcastle beamed at Wil. "Here are your artifacts, Dr. Wilson."

Barry gestured to his camera, indicating he had everything he needed on film.

Congressman Jones told Wil, "Now's your chance, boy!"

Wil wasn't quite sure what to do. This hadn't been the plan. He glanced at the team and met the eyes of Steve and Hope. Their nods of reassurance clarified the situation. Wil decided to start at the beginning and state the whole truth.

He stood in front of a cluster of microphones and cameras. He began, "About six weeks ago, when we were attempting to uncover some explosives hidden by terrorists in anticipation of the Secretary of State's visit to Israel, we discovered . . ."

Parenthood: No greater joy

no greater pain.

FATHERS

Hope and Wil opened their front door to greet Steve.

"What's this?" asked Hope as she accepted the bottle of champagne.

"I thought, since I wouldn't be here when the baby arrives, we might as well celebrate now."

Hope patted her stomach, smiling. At five months, she was beginning to show. She was moved by Steve's sentiment, though Wil was a little concerned about his pregnant wife drinking alcohol. He had read as much literature on prenatal care and mother/child health issues as he could get his hands on. He subtly liberated the bottle from Hope with a grin and started to mention that there was some nice juice she could have. But, before Wil could complete his task, Steve produced a bottle of sparkling cider with a bouquet of flowers.

"And these are for the mother."

Hope was now glowing.

After a hug and a handshake, Steve crossed the threshold. Wil brought Steve's suitcase and bag into the foyer as Steve retrieved a small package from his briefcase. Wil set the luggage down and Steve handed the package to his host.

"What's this?" asked Wil. It was cold to the touch and read, "Refrigerate after twenty-four hours."

"Anise-flavored sausage. Remember? You asked if I'd

237

make lasagna when I came to visit? I doubted I'd be able to find this kind of sausage in Jerusalem. It's the key to the recipe y'know."

Wil looked at his friend in disbelief and began to laugh. "And they let you through customs?!"

Hope said, "All I know is, I can hardly wait to taste it. It's become the standard to which Wil compares all Italian cuisine."

Wil took Steve's coat, and Hope led their guest into the main room of the house. On the way, Steve noticed a framed photo on Wil's desk. He picked it up.

"Is this from the wedding?" It was a picture of Hope and Wil standing in the snow with a woman Steve knew was Wil's mother.

"Yes," Hope replied. "We had a great time in Hazel Dell for Christmas. It was short and simple, but it was wonderful to see Wil and his mom rebuilding the bridges that had been torn down for so many years."

Steve was pleased to hear this. He set the photo down. He knew that reconciliation between Wil and his mother had begun, but it would take time.

Wil joined them and suggested that they sit and have some coffee. Hope went to the wet bar behind the sofa and picked up a freshly brewed pot of coffee before sitting next to Wil.

"Thanks." Wil took the coffee pot Hope handed him and began to fill the three cups on the little table in front of what used to be the only sofa in Wil's home.

"So, Hope, I see you haven't yet convinced this man it's okay to take some time off." Steve's glance took in the piles of research books and artifacts Wil had spread throughout the house.

"Nope." Hope placed her hand on Wil's knee. "And I'm not going to try."

"How was your flight?" asked Wil.

"A lot more relaxed than the one a year ago!"

Hope groaned in mock horror in memory of that trip.

"Actually, it was fine, though I'm glad I don't have to do that too often. When my congregation convinced me to lead this tour to the Holy Land, I had to remind them of how much I dislike long flights. Still, I'm glad I agreed to come."

Steve reached for his coffee cup. "How are you liking Israel, Hope?"

"I love it. I'm – umph . . ." The largest cat Steve had ever seen jumped into Hope's lap with a chewed-up red shoe dangling from its mouth. He had heard about this cat.

"Uh oh," Wil let slip out as Hope stood up, propelling Napoleon out of her lap and spilling her coffee.

"Napoleon!"

Wil jumped up and went to the wet bar. It wasn't clear if he was going for napkins to wipe up the spill or removing himself from a potential battle zone.

"Wil, I'm telling you! I'm going to skin this cat if he eats one more shoe!"

Hope was upset with Napoleon, but only a little. She grinned ruefully at the memory of this cat's escapades back in London. Hope's look softened her words and belied their meaning. She sat again and Napoleon climbed back into her lap as Wil wiped up the spill.

"He's still getting used to you – again. He'll eventually stop. Besides, it's obvious he likes you." And it was. The cat was snuggling and rubbing and purring his affection so much that it began to be slightly annoying.

Hope rolled her eyes. She remembered her promise to wait three more months before killing the cat if it didn't change.

"So anyway, Hope, you're liking Israel?" Steve tried to

get the conversation back on track, and Wil and his cat out of the hot seat.

"I really do like it – Israel, I mean." They laughed. "After the election, I wasn't sure what I was going to do. Newcastle's upset of Senator Brown made me want to end my political career batting 1000. When the *New York Times* offered me this position in Israel, it was . . . well, perfect. How could I say no?" Hope glanced in Wil's direction elfishly.

Nine months had elapsed since Steve performed their wedding, and he was delighted to see these two so happy.

"I'll bet you're glad to be back at the Institute and finished with those congressional hearings, eh, Wil?"

"I'll say!" Wil leaned back and put his arm around Hope. "It was phenomenal to see how the tone changed after our 'adventure.' Being in the middle of the squabble between Newcastle and Jones during the first part of the hearings was really unpleasant. Though they still aren't exactly peas in the same pod, they certainly pulled together during the second part. Best of all, it was a relief not to be the bad guy."

Steve concurred. "Watching Newcastle and Jones work together to expose the cover-up the President had orchestrated was fascinating, and even a little inspiring."

"It's still unsettling, though, that the President was pardoned by the man who beat him in the election," Wil added. "But it's sure nice all that's behind me."

Wil reflected for a few seconds and then lamented, "I still can't believe what a mess I made."

"But it all worked out," said Steve.

"And . . ." Hope touched Wil's hand on her shoulder. "At least one good thing came out of it."

Wil looked at Hope appreciatively before turning back to Steve.

"How's your job going? It sounds like your church membership is back up."

Steve nodded.

"And how do you have enough time to write your books? With all of your pastoral demands, I don't know how you do it." Wil's comment was in reference to Steve's latest book, which had come out a few weeks before his visit.

"Oh, I find the time. I have a great staff and it all works out." As much as Steve teased Wil for his long hours, Steve was also highly driven.

"You know, Steve, there's one thing I haven't been able to get past." Wil paused and reached for Steve's book on the desk behind him. "I still can't believe how you were able to take what I had thought was certainly going to be the death of Christianity and turn it into a best-selling Christian book."

"The fact that you found those other bones helped out a little, Wil," said Steve. "That's one of the reasons I dedicated it to you."

Hope smiled. Wil started to speak, but stopped.

"In fact, if it hadn't been for your second discovery, I wouldn't be here on this trip."

There was something ironic and funny about having a best-selling Christian book dedicated to an atheist whose goal in life had been to debunk Christianity.

"I also have you to thank for the story of the criminal's father," added Steve. "I couldn't get over the thought of that heartbroken man grieving over the loss of his baby girl, his beloved wife, and then his son, whom he watched die on a cross. When I think about it, it almost brings tears to my eyes." Steve paused.

"When we lost our son in the car accident, I could hardly bring myself to think about the pain William must have experienced when the car crashed."

Wil knew the loss of William had been especially difficult for Steve and Wendy.

"I know it was most likely over instantly, but the loss of a child is a horrifying thing for a parent. To watch your son die on a cross, as the father of the criminal who died next to Jesus had to, must have been unbearable."

"Do you really think there is a 'God the Father' who felt the same way as He watched Jesus die?" asked Hope. She had been moved by Steve's book.

"I do. Except, I believe God's pain was greater than anyone else will ever experience."

Wil resisted the conversation's shift toward the religious and wanted to bring it back to something more neutral. But he could see the thoughtfulness in Steve's eyes and remained silent.

"You see, many people have been unjustly killed on crosses," Steve continued. "Millions have been mercilessly tortured and murdered. But Jesus' greatest pain was not the physical agony. It was spiritual. As God, he was experiencing the complete rejection of the people he had created, loved, and come to give hope to. Jesus' greatest pain was the result of continuing to love the ones who were trying to destroy him. God could have stopped it. He could have destroyed humankind. Instead, he endured the pain and redeemed them.

"It wasn't the nails or the Romans or the Jewish leaders or us that kept Jesus on the cross. It was love."

Steve paused.

"God the Father allowed it to happen, knowing that His Son had willingly consented to the torturous death. I wouldn't have had the strength. It makes me realize how much the heavenly Father and his Son, Jesus, really care for us – *for all of us.*"

"But that assumes you believe Jesus is who he said he was," protested Wil. Over the past few months, Wil had done a lot of thinking on the meaning of the resurrection – if it were true – but he had not changed his position.

"That it does," acknowledged Steve.

"You know, Steve, I haven't given up my quest for the bones yet," Wil added, to ensure everyone knew he was still adamantly not a Christian. However, some of Wil's bitterness toward Christianity was beginning to fade and he had posed some thoughtful questions in recent e-mails to Steve.

"But Wil, what if you don't find the bones? *What if Jesus really did rise from the dead and if He really was who He said He was?*"

By the look on Wil's face, this question penetrated a little further than it had in the past. Looking at the resurrection objectively required a response he was not prepared to make. Not now. The conversation would continue – at another time.

"So . . . Steve, are you hungry?" Hope said to break the silence.

Wil picked up on the change of subject, which Steve conceded to. "We're having one of Hope's famous Greek salads," Wil said.

"But not until Oskar Gunderson and Beth get here," said Hope, who knew her husband was hungry and that he had the propensity to sample the main course before it was served.

"They were glad to hear you were coming, Steve. You know, they've become quite the number."

The three stood and headed to the kitchen. Steve put his arm around Hope and asked, "So, is it going to be a boy or a girl?"

"A boy!" said Hope and Wil in unison.

"A son. Wow! Hard to believe, isn't it Wil?"

Wil's joy was evident.

"Anyway, Steve," said Wil, wanting to resume the conversation on a subject that wasn't quite so personal. "Thanks for sending an autographed copy of your book to my mom. She was really . . ."

They walked into the brightly lighted kitchen as Napoleon followed, dragging the mangled shoe.

About the Author

Kevin Bowen is a Health Care Consultant who has a Master in Divinity, Master in Health Care Management and a Bachelor in History. He has lived in India, the corporate world, and the halls of academia. He now lives in the Victorian seaport of Port Townsend, Washington with his wife, two daughters, three cats and one bird.